to family that I have,

Morgan said to Callie.

His words stung. He cared about her like a *sister*. Callie's pride refused to allow her hurt to show.

Well, Callie hadn't asked him into her life. Her temper took control. "You've made it clear that you don't want to be here. If you honestly cared about my well-being it would be different. But your self-appointed guardianship is intolerable. Get out of my house and stay out!"

Morgan's jaw tensed. "Maybe I have been a little overbearing." He touched her cheek gently. "But you're wrong about one thing. I do care about you. I never want anything bad or unhappy to happen to you."

His fingers left a trail of fire. But it was the warmth in his eyes that truly shook her. There was an unmistakable protectiveness in those dark depths that shook her. He *did* care....

Dear Reader,

Aahh . . . the lazy days of August. Relax in your favorite lawn chair with a glass of ice-cold lemonade and the perfect summertime reading . . . Silhouette Romance novels.

Silhouette Romance books *always* reflect the magic of love in compelling stories that will make you laugh and cry and move you time and time again. This month is no exception. Our heroines find happiness with the heroes of their dreams—from the boy next door to the handsome, mysterious stranger. We guarantee their heartwarming stories of love will delight you.

August continues our WRITTEN IN THE STARS series. Each month in 1991, we're proud to present a book that focuses on the hero—and his astrological sign. This month, we feature the proud, charismatic and utterly charming Leo man in Kasey Michaels's *Lion on the Prowl*.

In the months to come, watch for Silhouette Romance books by your all-time favorites, including Diana Palmer, Brittany Young and Annette Broadrick. We're pleased to bring you books with Silhouette's distinctive blend of charm, wit and—above all—romance. Your response to these stories is a touchstone for us. We'd love to hear from you!

Sincerely,

Valerie Susan Hayward
Senior Editor

ELIZABETH AUGUST

A Small Favor

Silhouette Romance

Published by Silhouette Books New York

America's Publisher of Contemporary Romance

To Alice, my sister the nurse...
a profession I greatly admire.

SILHOUETTE BOOKS
300 E. 42nd St., New York, N.Y. 10017

A SMALL FAVOR

ISBN: 0-373-08809-4

First Silhouette Books printing August 1991

Books by Elizabeth August

Silhouette Romance

Author's Choice #554
Truck Driving Woman #590
Wild Horse Canyon #626
Something So Right #668
The Nesting Instinct #719
Joey's Father #749
Ready-Made Family #771
The Man from Natchez #790
A Small Favor #809

ELIZABETH AUGUST

lives in Wilmington, Delaware, with her husband, Doug, and her three boys, Douglas, Benjamin and Matthew. She began writing romances soon after Matthew was born. She'd always wanted to write.

Elizabeth does counted-cross stitching to keep from eating at night. It doesn't always work. "I love to bowl, but I'm not very good. I keep my team's handicap high. I like hiking in the Shenandoahs as long as we start up the mountain so that the return trip is down rather than vice versa." She loves to go to Cape Hatteras to watch the sun rise over the ocean.

Elizabeth August has also published books under the pseudonym Betsy Page.

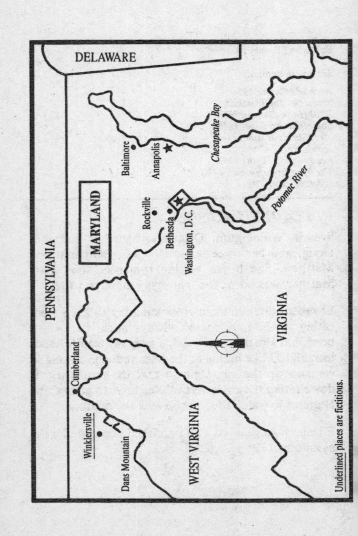

DELAWARE

PENNSYLVANIA

MARYLAND

Cumberland

Winklersville

Dans Mountain

WEST VIRGINIA

Rockville

Bethesda

Washington, D.C.

Baltimore

Annapolis

Chesapeake Bay

Potomac River

VIRGINIA

Underlined places are fictitious.

Chapter One

He was back. Callie had told herself that she could handle this. But seeing him again was much more difficult than she ever could have imagined it would be. He looked a great deal different than he had the first time she'd seen him. That time he'd arrived wearing jeans, a sweatshirt and sneakers...clothes Doc had bought for him.

Today he arrived in a tailored, gray pin-striped suit, which probably cost more than her entire wardrobe, Italian leather shoes, a silk tie and a handmade shirt. And instead of being driven in Doc's old station wagon, he'd come in a rented silver Mercedes. The white-haired woman with him, Callie knew, because of the arrangements that had been made, was his secretary, Janice Sagory.

Callie watched him as he opened the trunk and began taking out luggage, her mind flashing back several months to the day Doc had first approached her about John Smith. John Smith wasn't his real name. At that time they hadn't known his real name. He'd been in a car accident. The police weren't certain how it had happened, and at that time John hadn't been able to tell them. All anyone knew was that John Smith's car had gone off the road and plunged into a twenty-foot ravine. He'd either been thrown free or had somehow managed to get out of the car before it caught fire and exploded. His wallet and any other identification he had been carrying had been left in the car. He'd been wearing blue jeans and a broadcloth shirt that could have been purchased at any number of stores anywhere in the country. There had been a gold money clip in his pocket with five hundred dollars in it. But that was all. Thus, there was nothing to identify him with.

A little over a week after the accident Doc had come to see her. "Got a problem," he'd said.

Problem was a definite understatement, Callie mused in retrospect. In her mind's eye, she could see Doc standing there in front of her with that coaxing expression on his face...the one he always used when he wanted a really big favor from her....

"You remember that accident victim I told you about," he'd continued. "I've got to get him out of the hospital in Cumberland. He's driving the nurses crazy. They're threatening to quit if I don't order him put under total sedation for the next two weeks."

Callie couldn't help smiling. Dr. Howard Marsh, tall and lanky with a thinning head of steel-gray hair, had been ministering to the population of Winklersville for better than forty years. When her mother had refused to go to the hospital for Callie's birth, Doc had delivered Callie right here in this house. But more than that, he'd been Callie's friend and he was as close to a father as she'd ever known. "And so you want to bring him here and let him drive me crazy."

"Thought you could use a little extra income, what with the factory laying you off. And you could use the company." He placed a fatherly arm around her shoulder. "I've been worried about you spending so much time alone in this big old house since your grandma died."

"You really don't have to worry about me," she assured him. They'd had this talk before, right after her grandmother's funeral. Doc had suggested that she spend some time with her mother and stepfather but she'd refused. They had their own lives to live and five other children to feed and clothe. But more than that, she knew her presence caused her mother embarrassment. Besides, she was used to being on her own.

"All right, I won't worry about you." Doc gave her shoulder a little squeeze, then released her. "But I *am* worried about my patient. The injury to his eyes is going to take another couple of weeks to heal, but other than that he's perfectly healthy. He needs a quiet place with someone who can give him the kind of attention a blinded person requires. Since we don't know who he is, the state has had to accept responsibility for him for now. You won't get much compensation, but you'd be helping a fellow human being."

Callie would have done anything for Doc. He'd always been there for her when she'd needed a friend.

But she wasn't too certain about taking a stranger into her home. "How do you know this guy isn't a mass murderer or, at the very least, a thief?"

Doc rubbed his chin in a thoughtful manner. "The police ran his prints through every file in the country and looked through every wanted poster they had. They couldn't find any record on him."

Still Callie hesitated. She could use the money but she didn't need it, not yet anyway. "I don't know."

"I wouldn't ask you to do anything I thought would put you in danger," he coaxed. "John's a good man. He's just frustrated and, although he won't admit it, he's scared, too. The specialists have assured him that his eyes will heal, but until he can actually see again, he's going to worry. That, coupled with his loss of memory, would make anyone edgy. He needs to be out of the hospital. He should be somewhere where he has something other than his problems to keep his mind occupied. I'd take him into my home, but I'm never there."

Callie had never been able to refuse Doc when he had his mind set on something, and it was clear he was determined about this. She breathed a resigned sigh. "All right."

Doc smiled brightly. "I'll have him here by dinnertime," he promised, already heading for his car as if he was afraid that if he stayed a moment longer she would change her mind.

"I'll fix a pot roast. You might as well stay and eat," she called after him.

"I was counting on you asking me to," he yelled back as he slid into the driver's seat.

Callie caught a flutter out of the corner of her eye. Chester! "And you'd better behave yourself," she snapped over her shoulder. There was only empty air behind her but she'd expected that. Chester didn't show himself very often, which was just as well. Ghosts made most people nervous.

Doc arrived around four o'clock with John Smith in tow. Callie hadn't expected them for another hour. They found her in her garden, weeding. "Got an emergency," Doc explained hurriedly. "Helen Jenkins is having her twins. Just have time to drop John off."

Callie had barely gotten to her feet and removed her gloves, when Doc handed her a small satchel and started walking away. "I'll be back tomorrow to find out how the two of you are getting along," he said without looking back.

Callie stood dumbly holding the satchel and staring at the man in front of her. He stood around six foot two. His thick brown hair looked freshly cut. As if to give proof of this observation a whiff of talc reached her nostrils. Doc must have taken him by a barbershop on their way here, she concluded, wondering if Mr. John Smith normally wore his hair in such a conservative cut. It suddenly dawned on her that even Mr. Smith wouldn't know that. It had to be unnerving not to remember anything about your life. She recalled Doc saying that he was sure his patient was scared. But studying her guest she found it difficult to picture him being afraid. His jaw was square and strong and set in a determined line. The sweatshirt he wore fitted comfortably over broad shoulders and his stance was straight and firm.

"They call me John Smith," he said, breaking the silence between them as the sound of Doc's car faded in the distance.

Callie wiped her palm on her jeans to dry the sweat left from her gloves and shook his outstretched hand. "Callie Benson." His hand was as strong as the rest of him looked, but the palm was smooth. He was not a man who had made his living by manual labor. "Guess we'll have to get acquainted on our own." There was a heat from his touch that was spreading up her arm and causing a curious curling sensation in the pit of her stomach. Nerves, she told herself. She was allowing a strange man to move into her home. Any woman would be tense. She freed her hand quickly.

"Where exactly are we?" he asked, turning his head in a scanning motion as if he could actually see beyond the bandages that covered his eyes.

"We're on the outskirts of Winklersville, Maryland, on the west side of Dans Mountain," she replied. "East of Barton and south of Cumberland. I've got twenty acres here, mostly wooded land."

He shrugged as if the names of the towns meant nothing to him. "Guess it doesn't matter," he muttered. He suddenly smiled crookedly. "I believe I should be thanking you for rescuing me from the hospital."

He had a nice smile, a really nice smile. "I owed Doc a favor," she replied, feeling unexpectedly shy. "He likes you."

"I like him." The smile became a frustrated frown. "It's been damned scary not knowing anything about myself. He's been a real friend."

It surprised Callie to hear his admission of fear. Most of the men she knew would never make an open confession like that. "Doc's a good person."

John Smith's face was positioned as if he was looking at her. "You must trust him a great deal to allow him to talk you into taking a complete stranger into your home."

It was curious. She knew he couldn't see her. Still, she could feel him studying her. "I do trust him," she replied. Too tense to continue to stand there, she took a step toward her guest. "I think it's time for me to show you around. Right now you're facing my vegetable garden, or what will *be* a vegetable garden," she corrected. It was spring and the new plants were just now beginning to grow.

"Seems to work best for guiding if you hold on to my elbow," he said, bending his arm to give her an angle to hold.

As her hand fastened firmly upon him, she could feel the strong musculature beneath the sweatshirt he wore. Doc had better be right about Mr. Smith being safe to have around, she thought. At the moment she felt anything but safe. The rush of heat she had experienced from his handshake was now spreading up her arm once again. *I'm simply overreacting because of nervousness,* she assured herself. Turning him to the right, she said, "The house is about fifty yards in front of us. The ground is a little uneven, so be careful."

"What's the house look like?" he asked as they walked toward it.

"It's a two-story white-frame in need of a fresh coat of paint. That's going to be my project this summer," she replied, noting that he walked with a firm step despite his blindness. "We're coming to the back porch." She slowed their pace. "It's four steps up to the door. The porch is fully enclosed. It runs along the entire length of the back of the house and is mostly filled with junk. It's sort of my catchall for tools and gardening supplies. There's an open porch on the front with a few chairs for sitting and a swing." As she spoke they had mounted the steps. Reaching across him, she opened the screened door. "You've got about ten feet to the kitchen door," she directed, retaining her hold on his elbow as he stepped onto the porch and she eased in beside him. The maneuver caused her body to brush lightly against his. Wherever they touched, she was acutely aware of the contact. *Stop this overreacting!* she ordered herself.

He moved his head around as if he were trying to see his surroundings. "Smells like something good is cooking."

"Pot roast," she replied, as they crossed the short distance and entered the kitchen. "It's Doc's favorite."

John smiled. "Smells like it could be mine, too."

Callie found herself hoping it was. *It's only natural to want to please a guest,* she told herself, startled by how strongly she wanted him to enjoy the dinner.

Slowly she began guiding him through the rooms downstairs. The concentration on his face told her he was trying to memorize the layout of the house on this single expedition.

"You're not the kind of person who shifts furniture around a lot, are you?" he questioned as he left her side and felt his way around the living room. There was agitation in his voice.

"No," she assured him.

"Good." In a voice close to a growl, he added, "In the hospital, people kept shifting the lounge chair in my room. I nearly busted my toe on it twice before I learned to move carefully until I discovered where they had put the damn thing."

Callie studied her guest. She wasn't certain what it was . . . the way he moved with his muscles tensed as if prepared to do battle with some unknown foe, or the way his mouth was set in a hard, defensive line, but he reminded her of a wild animal who had suddenly found himself caged and was searching for a way out. Sympathy for him flooded through her. "You've got to keep in mind that your condition is temporary," she said encouragingly.

"That's only true where my blindness is concerned," he corrected grimly. "The doctors aren't taking any bets that I'll ever regain my memory." His jaw tensed. "And even with the blindness, they tell me I'll be able to see again, but they can never be one hundred percent certain."

With an intensity that startled her, she sensed the fear and frustration behind his anger. Shocked by her empathy toward this stranger, she said, "I'm sure you'll be fine. Doc's not the kind of man to lead people on with false hope."

He drew a tired breath. "I'm counting on that."

The urge to reach out and gently stroke his jaw comfortingly was close to overwhelming. *Get a grip on yourself,* she ordered. *You barely know this man.* Aloud she said, "Shall we finish the tour?"

"Yes," he replied with a nod.

A few minutes later as they climbed the stairs to the second floor, she noticed him counting each step. "This isn't a large house, but your mind's still going to be a jumble if you try to memorize everything the first time around," she cautioned.

"Actually, I'm getting a very clear picture in my head. If I turn around and go back downstairs, the kitchen and dining room are to my right. The kitchen is large, the dining room only about half the size. On the other side of the hall is a small parlor toward the front of the house and in the back is a large living room. It's my guess you use the kitchen and living room on a daily basis and the dining room and parlor for guests."

Callie stared at him in amazement. He was right. "You're very perceptive."

"No, it's just that a lot of people arrange their homes like that. That way they have rooms that are neat for unexpected visitors and they don't have to go rushing around straightening up when they suddenly hear a car pulling up."

He spoke so matter-of-factly. Coming to a halt, she studied him. Maybe his memory was coming back. "Is that the way your home is arranged?" she coaxed.

He frowned in concentration, then shook his head. "I don't remember."

Again she felt his frustration and wished she hadn't asked. Silently she resumed their climb to the second-floor landing. "My room is the one to your right," she said as they reached the top of the stairs. A bout of nervousness at the thought of him roaming around among her things swept through her. There was no reason for him to go in there, she reasoned, choosing not to stop and guide him through it. "The room directly across the hall is another bedroom, but it's full of stored stuff I didn't feel like lugging up to the attic. The bathroom is next to it. Then there is a third small bedroom on that side," she explained as she led him toward the bathroom door.

"Second door on my left," he muttered as they came to a halt in front of the bathroom.

Standing in the doorway, Callie watched him as he felt his way around this room. "I've put you in the room next to mine on the other side of hall," she continued as he rejoined her and she guided him across the narrow hall. "There are only the two rooms on this side so they are larger."

"Second door on the right," he said, obviously concentrating. She could almost see his mind forming a layout of the rooms.

"That's correct," she confirmed.

He smiled crookedly. "I'll remember that. Wouldn't want to wear out my welcome."

There was an underlying seriousness in his voice and she knew this was a polite reassurance that he would behave himself. "I'd appreciate that," she replied, letting him know that she wanted him to keep his distance.

He nodded his understanding and she mentally breathed a sigh of relief. At least they had that settled between them.

"I don't mean to be pushy," he said, "but that dinner you have cooking is making me hungry."

She'd almost forgotten the food on the stove. Luckily it wouldn't burn from lack of attention. "I'll unpack your things, and then we can eat." They had entered his room and she set the duffel bag she had been carrying on the bed and unzipped it.

Reaching out, he caught her arm. "I need to do things for myself. You just tell me where I can put my stuff."

The imprint of his hand burned into her and she was acutely aware of the strength in his grip. A sudden rush of fear swept through her. It's just nerves, she admonished herself once again. She moved back slowly and he released her immediately. You see, he's perfectly safe, she assured herself. But safe wasn't an easy word to associate with her guest. Aloud, she said levelly, "The bureau is empty. You can use any of the drawers and there is a closet behind you."

Glancing over his shoulder as if he could actually see what she was describing, he nodded and smiled. "Thanks."

There was a polite note of dismissal in his voice, and taking the cue, she started toward the door. But in the doorway she hesitated, uncertain if she really should leave him alone. "I was thinking of making corn bread," she said for want of something better to say. "Do you like it?"

He turned in the direction of her voice and gave an impatient shrug. "I don't know."

Callie flushed. "Sorry," she apologized, angry with herself for reminding him of his amnesia.

"It's all right." He smiled crookedly. Then, as if reading her mind, he said again with dismissal, "I'll be all right. You run along."

Still she hesitated. "There's a large cowbell on the bedside table to your right. If you need me, ring it," she instructed, then added, "I'll come up for you as soon as I get the corn bread in the oven."

His smile was replaced by a scowl as his anger once again surfaced. "I don't like being babied. I didn't come here to be a burden on you."

Callie understood his frustration, but he had no reason to be angry with her. "I'm only trying to be helpful," she snapped. "Doc expects to find you in one piece when he comes by tomorrow." Now angry with herself for not controlling her temper, she decided that leaving would be the best solution. Turning, she started to step out into the hall.

"Miss Benson," John called after her, harsh apology in his voice. "I'm sorry. I didn't mean to sound so sharp. But I need to know that I can do things for myself."

She paused and turned back toward him. She could easily understand why the nurses had been anxious to have him gone. But she couldn't honestly fault him for trying to be independent. It was a trait that was important to her, too. "Guess we're both going to have a bit of adjusting to do," she said, adding in friendlier tones, "And call me Callie."

His smile returned. "Thanks. And you can call me John. I've sort of gotten used to the name."

His smile caused a current of pleasure to spread through her. Scowling at herself, she quickly left.

Down in the kitchen she continued to scowl as she checked on the roast, then began gathering the ingredients for the corn bread. Her life was a testimony to the destructiveness that resulted when a woman was vulnerable to a man's charm. Even more, she had been certain she was immune to any such weakness.

As she finished adding the last ingredient to the bowl, a flicker caught the corner of her eye. She glanced up and for a brief moment saw the image of a young boy who was dressed in a tattered uniform from an age long past. He was shaking his head at her as if questioning her sanity. Then he was gone. "I'm just feeling sympathy for Mr. Smith," she muttered defensively. "He's going through a rough time. I am most certainly not attracted to him. That would be stupid. I barely know him, and no one, not even Mr. John Smith, knows anything about John Smith."

Chapter Two

"Is there someone else here? Doc, did you make it for dinner after all?"

Startled by the unexpected male voice, Callie turned toward the door to see John entering the kitchen. "I would have come back upstairs to get you in a few more minutes," she said, wondering how much he had heard of what she had been saying. Her voice had been low and she hoped he hadn't heard anything distinctly.

"Don't worry, I didn't break anything of yours or mine on the way down," he assured her with a grin.

She started around the table toward him. "Let me guide you to a chair."

"Just tell me if I get too close to the stove." There was a warning note in his voice. It couldn't have been clearer if he'd actually said, "Don't come near me, I want to do this on my own."

"It's obvious why the nurses were ready to put you into a two-week sleep," she observed dryly, stopping in mid-stride.

"I didn't mean to sound ungrateful," he apologized gruffly. "It's just that I hate feeling helpless."

Even blind, she would never have thought of John Smith as being helpless. "The table is directly in front of you," she instructed. "When you reach it, there's a chair a little to your right."

"Thanks," he replied, his brow knit in concentration.

She watched him as he moved toward the table. His steps were cautious, but not hesitant. When he found the chair, he smiled with triumph, and she found herself smiling, too. Quickly she returned to making the corn bread.

John twisted his head slowly from side to side as if looking around the room. "You never answered my question. Is there someone else here?"

Callie glanced toward him. The man had enough on his mind without being told about Chester. Besides, he wouldn't believe in Chester's existence any more than Doc or anyone else, other than her grandmother, ever had. He'd probably think she was operating with one bolt missing. "There's no one else here," she replied. "I was just talking to myself."

"I only caught the tail end of what was being said but I thought I heard my name mentioned," he prodded.

"I was just wondering if you like your corn bread sweetened," she hedged. It wasn't a total lie. The thought had crossed her mind. "I generally leave the sugar out but I could add it."

He shrugged. "Make it the way you prefer it. Like I said before, I have no idea what I like."

Even in women? Callie wondered, then chided herself for the thought. Still, her gaze traveled over him speculatively. He had the kind of looks that would appeal to most of the women she knew. Including herself, she admitted. I've avoided men too long, she reasoned, frustrated that her mind kept returning to this train of thought.

Forcing her attention back to the corn bread, she finished mixing it, then poured it into the skillet that had been heating in the oven. As she closed the oven and set the timer to allow the bread to finish cooking, she said, "I thought we'd eat in the kitchen. I usually do."

"Sounds great to me," John replied. Callie had taken the pot roast out of the oven before she heated the skillet for the corn bread, and the aromas from the meat and vegetables were filling the room. "If your dinner tastes half as good as it smells, I'm going to love it."

Callie found herself smiling with pleasure. I'm simply pleased to have company that appreciates my cooking, she told herself. She'd have felt the same rush of delight if Doc had said that. But down deep she knew this was a lie. Doc had said the same thing many times and it hadn't caused her toes to want to curl. I've definitely been alone too long, she decided.

"Tell me about yourself," John requested, breaking the sudden silence that had fallen over the room.

The question caused a chill. She didn't like talking about herself. "There's not much to tell," she hedged. "Besides, I thought it was the man who was supposed to talk about himself."

"I definitely don't have much to tell," he countered. She was setting the table and a thoughtful expression came over his face as he followed her movements around the kitchen by the sounds of her actions. "Doc told me that you live here alone. He said this place belonged to your grandparents, but now they are both deceased."

"My grandfather died a couple of years ago and my grandmother passed away last year," she confirmed around a lump that suddenly formed in her throat.

"I'm sorry," he apologized. "I didn't mean to bring up a painful subject."

Callie looked at him. She had not thought her sorrow was that obvious. He was a better listener than most people. At least for the moment he is, she corrected her assessment, as it occurred to her that he was making up for his lost eyesight by concentrating on what people were saying and how they were saying it. "It isn't really painful," she replied. "I just miss them."

"But you have other family?" he prodded.

Callie's jaw tensed as she forced a casualness she did not feel into her voice. "Some, but I don't see them much."

"Any brothers and sisters?"

The man was full of questions! And she was in no mood to put on an act. "Between my mother and father, I have seven half brothers and half sisters," she answered, adding with a definite this-subject-is-off-limits tone, "I really don't like talking about myself."

"Now I have put my foot in my mouth," John muttered. A comradely sympathy entered his voice. "Sounds as if it must have been an ugly divorce and you got caught in the middle."

A bitterness swept through Callie. This was followed by a wave of self-directed anger. How could talking about her mother and father still cause such a sharp jab of pain? Neither had ever wanted to be a part of her life and she didn't want to be a part of either of theirs. Aloud she said stiffly, "You could say it was a difficult situation for everyone. My grandparents took me in and raised me. Now I'd really like to talk about something else."

For a long moment John remained silent. In spite of the fact that his eyes were bandaged, she again had the unnerving sensation that he was studying her. Her chin tightened. If he persisted, she'd tell him the whole truth. It would be embarrassing, but then she'd lived through a childhood of being teased and taunted and whispered about behind her back. Her skin was thick enough to handle his disapproval.

The muscles around John's mouth moved as if he was going to say something, then stopped himself. Abruptly his jaw relaxed. "I shouldn't have pried. It was impolite." Suddenly a smile played at the corners of his mouth. "Why don't you tell me what vegetables you're raising in that garden of yours and I'll see if any of the names spark my memory."

Callie took a deep breath and forced herself to relax. It was stupid to let herself get uptight about her family history. He'd only been asking because he was looking for something to talk about. He wasn't really interested. "String beans, broccoli, spinach, carrots, onions, leaf lettuce, corn, potatoes and tomatoes," she ticked off, glad for the change of subject.

He gave a low whistle. "I thought you were talking about a small kitchen garden. That sounds pretty extensive."

"My grandparents raised nearly everything we ate. I still do," she replied matter-of-factly as she lifted the pot roast out of its pan and put it on a platter. "I've got some chickens, too, and a couple of apple trees."

"Guess that helps a lot," he mused thoughtfully. "Doc said you'd been laid off from your job at the factory in Cumberland."

Callie's back stiffened. She'd faced prejudice with pride but pity was something she couldn't tolerate. "I can do just fine without the job," she assured him. "My grandparents left me this place free and clear. There is also some insurance money, and I live real cheap."

He frowned in the direction of her voice. "Seems like somewhere I've gotten onto the wrong track. I don't seem to be able to say anything that's right."

Mentally Callie chided herself. She had overreacted. "Now it's my turn to apologize," she said. "If the factory doesn't start rehiring soon, I think I'll go find myself a job as a waitress or something. It's obvious I've been spending too much time alone. Guess I've forgotten how to carry on a polite conversation."

The frown faded and the thoughtful expression returned to John's face. "And I didn't mean to pry. I know it's got to be difficult to have a stranger living under your roof. I've just been trying to get acquainted.''

She was already having some very uncomfortable reactions to Mr. John Smith. Becoming better acquainted could be a very bad idea, a little voice in her head warned. ''Maybe it would be better if we just stayed strangers,'' she suggested firmly.

His frown returned. ''Maybe,'' he conceded.

For the next few minutes, a heavy silence hung over the room while Callie made gravy, and the corn bread finished cooking. But as she set the food on the table and saw the grim expression on John's face, she knew she'd behaved badly. ''We seem to be having some trouble finding a middle ground,'' she said levelly. ''I didn't mean to sound unfriendly. It's just that you make me nervous.'' She flushed scarlet when she realized the admission she had made. Quickly trying to cover this slip of the tongue, she added, ''Like you said, I'm not used to having a stranger suddenly living under my roof.''

His jaw relaxed. ''I can understand that. I've been surrounded by strangers ever since I woke up in the hospital. It is unnerving. But I promise I don't bite. I might growl every once in a while, but I'm not dangerous.''

Dangerous was exactly how she would describe him, Callie thought as he smiled quirkily and a rush of heat raced through her. Frowning at herself, she turned her attention to filling his plate. But as she picked up a knife with the intention of cutting his food, she stopped herself. "Shall I cut your food or is that another thing you're determined to do on your own?"

"You'd better do the cutting," he conceded, adding gruffly, "But I can feed myself. I hate having someone spoon food into my mouth. I can never get the right rhythm. The aides who came in to feed me were always trying to feed me too fast or too slow. And it grated on my nerves to have someone watching my every bite."

Callie had this sudden mental picture of the nurses and aides armed with ropes and gags descending on Mr. John Smith, and her sympathies were with them. "They were only trying to be helpful."

He rubbed the back of his neck. "I realize that, and I'm sure I was a royal pain. But this not knowing who I am, what I am, where I come from, if I have a family somewhere that's worried about me...it gnaws at me." His jaw tensed. "Sometimes I feel as if I can almost remember. There's this little flash of light like a dark cloud parting to let the sunshine through, then suddenly it's gone."

The frustration in his voice tugged at her heart, and Callie had the strongest urge to wrap her arms around his shoulders and give him a comforting hug. Instead she settled for saying "Maybe you're trying too hard. I'm sure if you relax and just give yourself time to get over the trauma of the accident, you'll remember."

He rubbed his neck harder in an outward sign of increased agitation. "Maybe I'm afraid to remember. Maybe I've done something too terrible to remember."

"I thought about that myself," she admitted honestly, then swallowed back a gasp when she realized what she'd said.

"And yet you allowed me to come into your home?" he demanded.

The sharp reprimand in his voice caused her shoulders to stiffen defensively. He was benefiting from her willingness to take this chance, and yet he was admonishing her for her action. "Doc thinks you're safe to have around and I trust him."

"That's lucky for me." Again he focused his attention on her as if he could actually see her. "I swear I won't do you any harm."

Callie believed him. She wasn't certain why. Maybe it was the set of his jaw or the resolve in his voice. *Or maybe I just want to believe him, and this will turn out to be the stupidest thing I've ever done,* her cautious side interjected. Aloud she said, "Your dinner is ready." She set his plate in front of him. "The meat is directly in front of you. The carrots are to your left and the potatoes are to your right." A thought suddenly stopped her. "Do you remember which is your left and which is your right?"

He nodded. "I also remember what the face of a clock looks like. You can give me directions using that. I can even remember who the president is." Again frustration filled his voice. "I can remember all kinds of nonessential information but I can't remember a damn thing about me."

Callie had rounded the table to place his plate in front of him. Now she was standing beside his chair. Without realizing what she was doing, she put her hand on his shoulder. "I'm sure you'll remember soon."

Reaching up, he covered her hand with his own. "Thanks," he said gruffly.

It was a friendly gesture, but the strength of her awareness of the firm feel of his shoulder beneath her palm and the warmth of his large hand over her smaller one caused her whole body to tense. I'm over-reacting to the situation, not to him, she told herself once again as she eased her hand free. Still, she decided that it would be best to keep any physical contact to a minimum. Going back to her chair on the other side of the table, she seated herself. "Would you like some corn bread?" she offered, determined to keep their conversation on impersonal ground for the rest of the evening.

"Yes, please," he replied.

Callie tried to concentrate on her own meal but found herself constantly glancing toward him.

"How am I doing?" he asked, suddenly breaking the silence between them.

She was slightly embarrassed that he had guessed she was watching him. "Very nicely," she replied.

He rewarded her with a smile. "You're a good cook. I wouldn't want to waste any of this by dropping it."

A glow of pleasure enveloped Callie. Disconcerted by the strength of her reaction to this compliment, she shifted her gaze to the window behind him. Dusk had arrived. Anxiousness replaced the warm glow his compliment had brought, and she realized that she had hoped Helen would have her twins quickly and Doc would show up to ease the way through this first evening. It was silly to be apprehensive just because it was getting dark, she chided herself. When she'd agreed to this arrangement, she'd known John Smith would be spending the nights here in her home. But somehow it hadn't quite sunk in until now.

"What color is this room?"

Callie's muscles had been tensing again, and the unexpected sound of John's voice caused her to jump slightly. "What?"

"I was just wondering what color the room is," he repeated.

"The walls and ceiling are white. The cabinets are oak, but stained with a walnut finish. My great-grandfather made them. The curtains are blue with pink flowers. I made them," she rattled off. She knew she was talking too quickly but she couldn't stop herself. "The table we are sitting at is pine. My grandfather made it for my grandmother the year they were married. He also made the chairs. They're not the most elegant you'll ever see, but they're sturdy."

"Your grandfather was a carpenter?" he questioned conversationally.

"No." Callie shook her head. "He worked at the glass factory, but he liked working with wood, too. That was his hobby. He made my bed and the bed in your room." She scowled as a slight catch sounded in her voice at the mention of the beds. *You're acting like a nervous adolescent,* she chided herself. *Calm down.*

But John Smith didn't seem to notice. "What color is the living room?" he prodded.

During the rest of the meal, she described the color scheme of the house to him. She did notice that he skipped asking her about her bedroom. Studying him, she knew he had heard the nervous catch in her voice earlier, and this was his subtle way of reassuring her that he had no intention of intruding on her privacy. Once again she began to relax.

Following the meal she accompanied her guest into the living room, got him comfortably seated and handed him the remote control for the television. Once she was satisfied he could operate the control, she left him and returned to the kitchen to clean up the dishes.

As she worked she had a stern little talk with herself about being overly sensitive to having a man around. By the time she had the dishes washed and the kitchen back in order, she was feeling in total control of her world once again.

"I have a favor to ask."

Callie swung around to find John standing in the doorway. *Relax!* she ordered herself. "Yes, what is it?"

"This haircut is itching. I need my hair washed but I'm not supposed to get my eye patches wet." He shifted slightly, his embarrassment obvious. "I was wondering if you'd help me."

"Sure, no problem," she replied. What could she do? She couldn't say no. She wasn't going to admit that he made her so nervous she didn't want to touch him. That would sound ridiculous. It *was* ridiculous!

"You'll have to take off the outer wrapping," he directed, his hand going up to touch the ring of gauze wrapped over his eyes and around his head. "I've got another roll of gauze upstairs to replace it when we're finished. There are inner bandages on both eyes. You can cover each one with a folded piece of gauze and tape that in place. Doc sent a roll of tape along, too. That'll keep the inner bandages in place until we're finished."

Mentally Callie debated between using the bathroom sink or the kitchen one. The bathroom would be very cramped, she decided. "The kitchen sink would probably be the best place," she said, wishing Doc would drive up at that moment and offer to help his patient. But he didn't. *Just get it over with,* she ordered herself. "I'll go get the gauze, tape, shampoo and a couple of towels," she tossed over her shoulder, already moving toward the kitchen door.

When she returned, she found John sitting at the table. He was in the process of removing the outer bandage. Quickly taking over, she finished the unwrapping. While he held the inner bandages in place, she cut and folded two squares of gauze, then after placing them over the inner bandages, secured them in place with the tape. She tried to think of what she was doing but his skin felt warm and inviting, and the desire to run her finger along his jawline taunted her. Stop it! she ordered herself and stepped away from him. "I don't think I have a chair that's high enough for you to sit and lean back in," she said, picking up a hand towel and folding it into a thick pad. She placed the pad in his hand. "But if you hold this over your face and I wash carefully, I think we can do this with you standing leaning forward."

He nodded and, rising from the chair, allowed her to guide him to the sink.

Carefully Callie wetted his hair and applied the shampoo. She had tried to steel herself against any reaction to him but she had not considered the extent of the close proximity in which she would have to work. She was forced to stand with her leg and side against him and as she bent over him, her breast brushed against his back, his shoulder and his arm. Wherever there was contact, a heat penetrated her clothing. It was like resting on a sun-scorched boulder on a hot July day, she thought as the warmth spread through her.

Your body is behaving irrationally, her inner voice shouted. *And dangerously,* it added warningly. *Think of him as an inanimate object and concentrate on washing his hair.* She tried but it didn't help. His hair was thick and the texture enticing to her touch. Her gaze traveled to his neck. The suds were working their way down onto it. Scooping them up, her palm trailed along the strong, hard cords, and an excitement stirred within her. Her whole body seemed sensitized to his, and she was experiencing a curiously warm curling sensation in her abdomen. *Just get this over with,* she ordered herself, thoroughly shaken. "Are your bandages staying dry?" she asked stiffly, again trying to keep her mind only on the business at hand. But then it wasn't her mind that was causing her so much trouble. It was her body.

"So far so good," he replied.

Her jaw set in a determined line, she worked carefully, but quickly, to finish.

"Done," she announced at last, wrapping a towel around his head and beginning to dry his hair.

John dried the edges of his face thoroughly, then laid the hand towel aside and straightened. Trying to keep the towel in place on his head, Callie found her body brought into even firmer contact with his. Her breath locked in her lungs.

"I can dry my hair now," he said, his fingers colliding with hers as he reached up to take over the towel.

"Yes, fine," she managed, quickly relinquishing the job to him and taking a step back. Watching as he rubbed vigorously, she took several deep breaths. After all of these years of being so practical where men were concerned, how could she let a total stranger affect her this way? By tomorrow I'll be back to normal, she promised herself.

Satisfied his hair was dry enough, John laid the towel aside. Taking a comb from his pocket, he combed his hair.

"I shouldn't put the outer bandage back on until the hair is completely dry," Callie said, watching him check the dressings that were in place to make certain they were still secure and dry. "I've got a hair dryer upstairs. I'll just go get it and finish the job."

Ten minutes later she had his hair completely dry. But when she started to remove the makeshift outer bandages in order to replace them with the fresh wrapping of gauze, he stopped her.

"I hope I don't sound like a nuisance. But I'd like to take a bath first," he requested.

Callie regarded him in horror. She, most definitely, wasn't going to wash his back.

"If you'll just show me how the tub works, I can manage on my own," he continued as if reading her mind.

Callie nodded, then, realizing he couldn't see her, she said, "Sure," and marveled at how casual the word sounded considering how shaken this last request had left her.

She accompanied him upstairs. Once there, she got out a fresh towel and washcloth for him and hung them on the rack at the end of the tub. Succinctly she explained which tap was for the hot water and which for the cold. Then she handed him the rubber stopper and started backing out of the bathroom. But at the door, she paused. "There's a hamper against the wall." She took his hand and placed it on the object in question. "You can put your clothes inside—". she opened the lid to demonstrate what she meant "—and I'll wash them."

"Thanks," he replied, setting the stopper on the edge of the tub and reaching for the hem of his sweatshirt.

Callie completed her exit quickly. But out in the hall, she stood indecisively looking at the closed bathroom door. She wanted to go downstairs and put her guest out of her mind for a while, but she couldn't. She was worried he might slip and fall and need help. So she remained standing, leaning against the hall wall opposite the bathroom.

A flicker caught the corner of her eye and then was gone. Chester again. Apparently having a stranger in the house made him nervous, too.

Callie watched the door anxiously, all the time hoping John Smith would not require her services. Periodically she heard water swishing, giving proof that her guest was fine. Still she remained anxious.

Finally the door opened. Callie's teeth closed over her bottom lip as he stepped out into the hall with only the towel wrapped around his hips for covering. Her gaze traveled over his broad chest, then followed the vee of dark curly hair downward to his hard, flat abdomen. She felt a flush building, but she couldn't stop herself. Her gaze continued downward to the sturdy columns of his legs. She noted the bruises and scrapes left by the accident. He was truly lucky to be alive and in such good shape. And, he was in good shape. She considered remaining perfectly quiet. Maybe he wouldn't realize she was there. But that didn't seem fair. "If you'd have asked, I'd have gotten you your robe," she said evenly.

His hand tightened its hold on the towel and she saw a flush that matched her own darken his neck and face. He was shy. That made her own embarrassment less intense.

"Doc forgot that item," he replied, moving down the hall toward his room.

Callie ordered herself to stop watching him and go in and straighten the bathroom but her legs and eyes refused to obey. He was very nice to look at. A sudden wave of self-directed anger shook her. How could she behave so wantonly? She, of all people, knew the dire consequences such behavior could cause.

Furious with herself, she jerked her attention away from him and stalked into the bathroom.

Chapter Three

In the middle of straightening the bathroom and having a very stern talk with herself, Callie remembered her grandfather's robe. Virgil Benson hadn't been quite as tall as her guest but he had been a large man. She guessed his robe would fit Mr. Smith. It was the only article of her grandfather's clothing left in the house. All the rest had been given to charity. But her grandmother had kept the robe, and every once in a while Callie would find Ruth Benson wrapped in the old flannel garment, curled up in her husband's chair.

"Wearing this old thing makes me feel closer to him," she'd told Callie. "It helps me cope with the loneliness."

After her grandmother passed away, Callie had kept the robe. She'd planned to give it away along with her grandmother's clothing. But instead she'd pulled it out of the box at the last moment and washed it and put it away. She'd never actually understood why she'd done it. She just had.

"But now I do have a use for it," she muttered.

Giving the bathroom a nod of approval, she went and got the robe.

"Just a minute," came the barked reply to her knock on John's door. When the door opened, he was standing there barefoot wearing a fresh pair of jeans and a sweatshirt. "Must have left my shoes in the bathroom," he said tersely.

Callie had the distinct feeling he was still embarrassed from the towel episode. "You did," she confirmed. She had set the shoes in the hall just outside his door before going to look for the robe. Now she picked them up. "Here they are," she said, handing them to him. "And I brought you something else." The flush returned to her face. "A robe."

"Thanks." A tint of pink came to his cheeks as he laid the shoes aside and accepted the garment.

An uneasy silence threatened to settle between them. *Get a grip on yourself,* Callie chided mentally. She was an adult. Even watching TV movies, she'd seen more than he'd exposed. She'd just never seen it quite so...personally. "How about if I replace that outer wrapping over your eyes now?" she suggested.

"I can do it, but thanks for the offer," he replied. A frown knit his brow. "Guess everything's still in the kitchen."

She shook her head at his stubborn determination. "I'll go get what you need," she said, heading for the door to retrieve the necessary articles from the kitchen. Hearing him moving behind her, she glanced over her shoulder expecting to find him following her. She half expected him to insist on going down to the kitchen by himself. But instead he was making his way to the chair on the far side of the bed. He refused to grope with his hands, and she heard the sharp intake of breath and the muttered curse when he stubbed his toe on the corner of the chest at the foot of the bed. But she made no move to help him. He wouldn't appreciate it. The man had a decidedly independent streak.

When she returned, she found him seated and waiting.

"Guess you might do a better job," he said grudgingly, as she approached him.

It was obvious he didn't like asking for help, but then she'd never been any good at that, either. "I really don't mind doing it," she assured him, as she set aside the scissors and began unwrapping the gauze.

"I don't like to feel as if I'm a burden," he said self-consciously. Clearing his throat, he added with an edge of hostility, "And there was no reason for you to wait outside the bathroom."

His embarrassment had turned to anger. Well, she couldn't blame him. She'd probably feel the same if their roles had been reversed. "I apologize for invading your privacy," she replied, adding in her defense, "but I was worried that you might slip and fall."

For a moment his scowl persisted, then the corners of his mouth relaxed. "I suppose in your place I would have done the same," he admitted. A sudden mischievous grin spread across his face. "Can't help wondering if I would have enjoyed the view."

Callie stiffened. She never played flirtatious games. They only led to trouble. "That's a question that will have to go unanswered."

"Fair's fair," he persisted. "I know you have a nicely feminine figure. I could feel the curves when you were washing my hair."

The approval in his voice sent a current of pleasure shooting through her. *Don't be a fool!* she chided herself. *You know better than to let a little flattery go to your head.* "My curves are really none of your concern," she said coolly. She had finished the bandaging. Setting the gauze and scissors aside, she turned and strode toward the door.

"Callie?" He had risen to stop her but as he took a long step, his toe hit the bedpost. "Damn!" he cursed, sucking in a sharp gasp of pain.

Immediately she regretted having caused him to hurt himself. "Are you all right?" she asked anxiously.

"In my condition, what's one more broken bone?" he muttered, sinking onto the edge of the bed and lifting his foot to feel the damage.

A part of her wanted to help him, but a stronger part kept her near the door. She'd felt the sharp jab of pain as if it was her own and this scared her. She needed distance between herself and this man. "I don't think it's broken," she offered, watching him wiggle the digit.

"No," he conceded. Then, forgetting about his foot, he turned his head in the direction of her voice. "I didn't mean to upset you. I was just trying to make a little light conversation."

Callie drew a deep breath. Why did she keep over-reacting? "I know, but I think it would be best if we kept our relationship strictly business."

He gave an indifferent shrug. "You're the boss."

The fact that he honestly didn't care stung. *But that's exactly what you expected,* she told herself, furious that she'd felt anything. "Now that that's settled," she said levelly, "is there anything I can do for you before I go back downstairs?" Her gaze traveled around the room as she spoke. It looked as if he'd put away what few possessions he'd brought with him. On the nightstand beside the bed, she saw an electric shaver. It was one of the self-charging kind. "I'll plug in your shaver," she offered, starting toward it.

"I followed the cord from the lamp and found the outlet," he replied.

Having taken a step toward the table, she could now see that the little red light was lit. "Guess you have everything under control," she observed. "So I'll just be on my way." In the next instant she was in the hall and closing the door behind her. "I wish I had myself under more control," she muttered as she went back downstairs. After all, he was just a man. But his presence did seem to fill the house.

I've definitely been spending too much time alone lately, she admonished herself once again.

Going into the living room, she switched on the television. Then, seating herself in the small wooden rocking chair that had been her grandmother's favorite, she picked up the afghan she was crocheting and began to work.

"Mind if I join you?"

Glancing toward the doorway she saw her guest entering the room. "No, of course not," she replied. It was silly of her to let his presence disturb her. She started to put her crocheting aside with the intention of leading him to a chair or the couch but as if he could read her mind, he held up his hand.

"Don't get up. I'll find my way," he said sharply, adding in a more level tone, "Just yell out if you think I'm going to break something."

"Yours or mine?" she questioned dryly, watching as he began to cautiously make his way across the room, using his feet and hands to probe for obstacles.

The firm set of his mouth relaxed into a momentary smile. "Either," he replied, then the look of concentration returned.

She only had to caution him once when it looked as if he might bump into a table holding an antique hurricane lamp. Mentally she made a note to remove it to the storage room after he'd gone to bed. It was an heirloom from her great-grandmother. Anything else in the room could be replaced if it was broken.

"Is there a show you'd particularly like to watch?" she asked after he'd sat down.

"Whatever you want to watch is fine with me," he replied with an indifferent shrug.

"Tonight's not one of my favorite viewing nights. I just switched it on for background noise while I crocheted. You choose." As she spoke she set her crocheting aside and rose. Handing him the remote, her hand brushed against his and a tingling sensation raced up her arm. Quickly she returned to her chair. Again picking up her crocheting, she tried to concentrate on the handiwork and ignore her companion. But she was unsuccessful. She found her attention shifting back to him as he panned through the stations and came back to the sit-com she'd had on. His restlessness was obvious.

Abruptly he switched the television off. "Do you mind if we just talk?" he asked, his voice close to a growl.

Setting aside her crocheting, she studied the taut line of his jaw. Every time they'd talked it had led to a confrontation. But she couldn't avoid conversation with him. Besides, he really did look as though he needed something to occupy his mind, and he had agreed to her ground rules. "What do you want to talk about?"

He shrugged. "Tell me about Doc. How old is he? What's he look like? Is he married? I'd just like to hear some normal conversation."

Callie didn't see any harm in acquiescing to this request. "Doc's fifty-six. Stands around six feet tall. He's lean as a willow...too lean if you ask me, but he eats like a horse. He has kind eyes but his nose looks like it belongs to a boxer. It's been broken a couple of times. The last time was by Sam Leary. Sam had been drinking and got himself into a brawl. He'd been knocked unconscious and Doc was called in to take a look at him. Doc was bending down over the patient when Sam came to. The problem was, Sam came to swinging and caught Doc with a right hook. Now Doc always makes certain he has two strong men holding down any drunk he works on."

She shook her head at the remembered picture of the doctor with his nose swollen and both of his eyes blackened. It hadn't fitted his image at all. "His hair is gray and he's balding on top." She smiled as she recalled the disgruntlement the doctor had expressed when he began to lose his hair. "I keep telling him that it makes him look distinguished. He's widowed. His wife died around six years ago. She had cancer. They never had any children so he sort of treats all of us who he delivered as his."

"I got the impression he considers you special," John interjected.

"I consider him special," she replied.

His mouth formed a self-conscious quirk. "What about me?"

Callie blinked in confusion. "What about you?"

The self-consciousness became more evident. "What do I look like?"

It hadn't dawned on Callie until this moment that he didn't know what he looked like. In his position she would have been curious, too. Her mind returned to the hallway upstairs and her guest wrapped in a towel. "You're a little over six feet tall and in good physical shape...not like a bodybuilder but firm." She flushed when she realized how outspoken she'd been. A light tint reddened his cheeks, too, and she quickly directed her attention to his face. "You have dark brown hair cut conservatively." She'd promised herself that she'd keep a distance between herself and her guest but her curiosity got the better of her. "Was that Doc's choice . . . the style of haircut, I mean?"

"Must be pretty close to the way I usually wear it," John replied. "Doc told the barber to only give me a trim."

Callie nodded. The cut suited him.

"Go on," he prodded when her pause threatened to lengthen into a silence.

Her gaze traveled along the hard line of his jaw. "I can't see your eyes but you've got a nicely shaped mouth for a man, and your nose fits your face. Your jaw line is firm and your teeth are straight. All in all, I suppose you could cause a woman to look twice."

He smiled crookedly. "But not you."

I might look, but I don't plan to touch, she answered mentally. Aloud she said, "I've always considered the man beneath the surface to be the most important."

His smile became a frustrated frown. "Can't help you there. I don't know what's beneath the surface." His jaw tensed. "How old do you think I am?"

Callie shrugged. "I'm not good at guessing ages. Doc seems to think you're in your early thirties. That seems about right to me."

His mouth formed a hard, straight line. "Guess that does it for me," he muttered. "What about you?" He held up a hand in a sign of peace. "I'm not trying to get personal, I just like to know what my surroundings are like."

"I'm twenty-seven, have brown hair, brown eyes, I'm around five feet, six inches tall . . . just sort of average looking," she replied.

He suddenly grinned. "You don't have a jealous boyfriend who's suddenly going to burst in here and break my nose so I'll look more like Doc?"

"No, you're safe on that count," she replied.

"Glad to hear that," he said with playfully exaggerated relief.

But the playfulness was surface thin. Callie watched him settle back in his chair, his expression becoming solemn as a silence descended over the room. Clearly he was bored. Well, she'd never been good at entertaining people. But in this instance she suddenly found herself wishing she could think of something to say. She told herself this wasn't because she didn't want to appear uninteresting. It was because she was certain he was again dwelling on his situation and she wanted to take his mind off it for a while. "We're having a real nice spring this year. Some years it seems to go directly from winter to summer...freezing one week and scalding the next."

You sound like a babbling idiot, she scolded herself. *The weather! He probably considers that more boring than silence.*

"It was pleasant today," he responded almost absently. "Of course, I wouldn't have minded a blizzard. I just wanted out of that hospital." He rose, then sank back into the couch. A self-mocking smile spread across his face. "I was going to pace. That could have caused some real destruction."

"I could clear you a path," she offered, again feeling his frustration as if it were her own.

He shook his head. "Thanks, but pacing doesn't help, either. I've tried that in the hospital." Leaning back on the couch, he started to stretch his legs out in front of him but they hit the coffee table and he immediately drew them back. "Hope I didn't knock anything off balance," he apologized quickly.

"You didn't," she assured him. "There's nothing on it but newspapers and magazines. You can just push it away with your feet if you want more legroom or you can use it as a footstool. I usually do."

"Thanks," he replied, lifting his legs and letting his feet come to rest, crossed at the ankles, on the short-legged table. Placing his hands behind his head, he leaned back farther and faced the ceiling. "Besides crocheting and watching television, what do you do for entertainment around here?"

"Play cards, go fishing, go into Cumberland for a movie or dinner once in a while," she rattled off, thinking how boring her life suddenly sounded.

"Cards are out and so is the movie and eating in public." Lifting his head, he turned toward her. "But if you can find the time, maybe we could try a little fishing?"

"Sure. We can go tomorrow," she agreed instantly. Startled by how eager she was to please him, her mouth formed a hard, straight line.

"Great!" He smiled with enthusiasm, then just as quickly the smile vanished. Leaning his head back, he again faced the ceiling and a seriousness descended over his features. "Have you ever been married?"

"No," she replied, her voice warning him that he was treading on soft ground.

John drew a deep breath. "Didn't mean to get personal," he apologized gruffly. A grimness entered his voice. "It's just that I can't help wondering if I have a wife and kids out there somewhere depending on me." Straightening, he turned toward her. "Do I look like a married man to you?"

The thought of him being married caused a hard little knot to form in her stomach. Ignoring it, she studied him. "I can't tell by the way a person looks if they're married or not," she replied honestly. "But you weren't wearing a wedding ring when you were found and your hands are evenly tanned which suggests you haven't worn one recently. Of course, not all married men wear rings." She regarded him apologetically. "Sorry I couldn't be of more help."

"You've been a big help. You let me come and stay in your home." Leaning back, he rubbed the back of his neck. "I think I would have gone crazy if I'd had to stay in that hospital another day." He grinned self-consciously. "It's very diplomatic of you not to add that the nurses felt the same way. I'll try to behave myself better here." He gave a self-conscious shrug. "I just feel so restless."

"I've noticed," she replied dryly.

"Sounds like I might be wearing my welcome a little thin already," he observed.

"No." The word came out too quickly. It sounded as if she enjoyed having him there. *And I don't,* she told herself. *I'm only doing this as a favor to Doc.* In a more level tone, she said, "I shouldn't be critical. I can understand your frustration."

He smiled. "You're a very kind lady."

His smile warmed her while his words made her feel spinsterish. *My emotions are bouncing around like*

Ping-Pong balls. I've got to get a grip on myself. What he thinks of me is of no importance. I'm simply his nursemaid for the next two weeks and that's all.

"I'm just doing Doc a favor. I owe him," she said stiffly, more to herself than for him.

His smile vanished. "Guess I ought to thank Doc then." Rising, he started cautiously toward the door. "But right now, I think I'll go to bed. It's been a long day."

Mentally Callie kicked herself. She'd sounded inhospitable. "I didn't mean that the way it came out. You really are welcome here."

His features relaxed. "Thanks. I know it can't be easy to suddenly have a total stranger in your house. It's not easy being a total stranger to everyone—including myself."

"You'll get your memory back," she said encouragingly.

Turning in the direction of her voice, he smiled crookedly. "I'm not sure I believe that, but it sounds good when people say it."

He added a good-night and she guided him around the table on which the hurricane lamp sat.

That crooked smile of his had again caused a warm curling sensation in the pit of her stomach. Determined to ignore it, she concentrated on her crocheting while she gave him time to get himself settled in for the night. Then, setting her handiwork aside, she rose and picked up the lamp. Carrying it upstairs, she placed it in her storage room for safekeeping. It took two more trips to bring up the rest of the things she didn't want harmed.

"Stashing all the valuables so they won't get broken?" A male voice greeted her as she left the room after her last trip.

Callie flushed with embarrassment.

"I hate being such a nuisance," he continued apologetically. "Sort of like having a two-year-old around, I guess."

Not at all like having a two-year-old around, she corrected mentally, her gaze traveling over him. "Just thought I'd save us both some worry," she replied evenly.

"Good idea," he returned. "'Night," he added. Reentering his room, he closed the door.

Callie drew a shaky breath. "Wish I could store my emotions away as easily," she muttered to herself as she went back downstairs to make certain all the lights were turned off. The way his smile caused a warmth to spread through her made her uneasy. "I'm just going through a little trauma getting used to having someone else in my home," she told herself firmly. "By tomorrow, he'll have little or no effect on me."

Chapter Four

"Callie? Chester said you were out here."

Callie's whole body went rigid. John hadn't been awake when she'd risen. Moving quietly so as not to disturb him, she'd made a pot of coffee, then taken her first cup of the day out onto the front porch. Sitting in an old wooden lawn chair her grandfather had made, she'd been watching the sun rise.

"Chester told you?" she choked out, swinging around as he joined her on the porch. Chester rarely talked to anyone—even her—and he *never* spoke to strangers. At least, not that anyone had ever mentioned to her.

John frowned. "You sound surprised, as if you didn't know he was here. Wasn't he supposed to be inside? Is he in the habit of going into people's homes uninvited?"

"I'm never sure when Chester is going to show up," she replied honestly. "I let him have free run of the place for the most part." An amused gleam came into her eyes as she recalled an incident years earlier. It had occurred around the time she had begun to notice her womanhood. Chester had come into the bathroom while she was bathing and she'd ordered him out. He was a polite enough ghost to have obeyed, and he'd respected her privacy ever since. Suddenly remembering her manners, she said, "There's a chair two paces to your right."

"Thanks."

Callie studied her guest as he made his way cautiously along the porch. Chester had actually talked to him. She still found that hard to believe.

"I suppose he comes over to do handyman work for you?" John said conversationally as he eased himself down into the chair.

"Handyman work?" she repeated. John Smith had already been through a lot. It didn't seem like a good idea to tell him he'd been conversing with a ghost. "Not exactly. He just sort of comes and goes. I suppose he looks at this place as his sanctuary," she hedged.

"He sounded young," John persisted.

Depends on how you look at it, Callie mused. Chester had been fifteen when he was killed at the battle of Shiloh, but that had been well over a hundred years ago. Aloud, she said, "He's fifteen."

John frowned thoughtfully. "That's a difficult age."

It certainly had been for Chester. "Yes," Callie agreed.

John's brow knitted into lines of concentration. For a long moment a heavy silence fell over the porch, then he drew a frustrated breath. "For a second there, I thought I might remember something about my childhood," he said disappointedly.

"I'm sure your memory will return soon," she said encouragingly. Then before he could bring up Chester again, she asked, "What would you like for breakfast... pancakes or eggs? How about some bacon?"

John shrugged. "You choose. Considering that hospital food is the only thing I can remember tasting besides your dinner last night, I've got no preference."

"Pancakes then," Callie decided. "They're Doc's favorite, and he said something about showing up this morning to check on you. He also likes bacon so I'll fry up some." As she rose and started into the house, she paused at the door. "Do you want to come in now?"

"Think I'll just sit out here," he replied, "And enjoy the fresh morning air."

He had stretched out his legs and encountered the porch railing. Lifting his legs, he'd settled his feet on the top rail. They were crossed at the ankles and he was leaning back in the old wooden chair. Callie couldn't help thinking that he looked comfortably at home. But this isn't his home and when the bandages come off, he'll be leaving, she reminded herself. In the kitchen, she glanced toward the coffee pot. It was only polite to take some out to him. Quickly she poured him a cup, added milk and carried it out to him.

"Thanks," he said as he accepted it from her. "But I'm not here so you can wait on me hand and foot," he added self-consciously.

"Actually, that is precisely why you are here," she replied. "And I don't really mind."

He smiled sheepishly. "Guess you're right, but I'll try not to be too much of a burden."

"You're not." What bothered her was that she was enjoying taking care of him. *It's only because I needed someone to take care of besides myself for a while,* she reasoned.

"Chester came out right after you left," John said as she started back inside. "I invited him to go fishing with us but he said he had something else he needed to do. He wasn't very specific."

Callie found herself wondering just what Chester did do when he wasn't around her, but now was not the time to speculate. "He keeps busy," was all she said, then she went on into the house.

As she mixed the batter for the pancakes, she wondered what Doc would say when she told him that his patient was talking to a ghost. While Doc had never questioned her sanity, she knew he wasn't convinced of Chester's presence. He treated her references to the boy the same way a parent would treat a child's talk toward an invisible friend...as if he expected that one day she'd forget about Chester and that would be the end of the ghost stories. However, she hadn't forgotten Chester as he'd expected and she knew that bothered Doc. He blamed her grandmother for encouraging her, because Ruth Benson had also claimed to see Chester. "And now Mr. John Smith has spoken with him," Callie muttered, an amused grin spreading over her face. That should shake Doc up a bit.

She had the bacon fried and was just about ready to begin cooking the first batch of pancakes when she heard Doc's car approaching. He'd always shown good timing when it came to a meal. And he knew his way to the kitchen. Not bothering to go out and greet him, she began to spoon the batter onto the griddle.

"Looks like I came by at the right time," he said, entering the kitchen just as the first batch was finished. He had John with him.

"Have a seat," Callie replied, nodding toward the table where she'd put out three place settings.

"Your chair's two steps straight ahead," Doc directed, releasing John's elbow. Then, letting his gaze travel to the food on the stove and back to the table, he grinned broadly. "My favorite."

"You said you'd be here this morning, and I figured you'd try to make it for breakfast," Callie replied, setting a plate of pancakes at each man's place. As she returned to the stove, she asked over her shoulder, "How's Helen?"

"Has two healthy boys," Doc replied. "Six pounds, one ounce and six pounds, five ounces."

"She must be feeling a lot lighter," Callie remarked, her mind only half on the new arrivals as she watched John finding his seat.

"Lighter, but with her hands full," Doc replied, also keeping an eye on his patient.

"Do you remember what pancakes look like and how you eat them?" Callie asked as John positioned himself in front of his plate.

He frowned, then he smiled. "I seem to recall that they require butter and syrup." Abruptly his frown returned. "It's crazy. I can remember what pancakes are but I can't remember my own name."

"It will all come back with time," Doc assured him.

The frown became a self-conscious quirk. "Maybe you or Callie had better do the buttering and syrup-pouring," John requested.

Callie had carried Doc's coffee to the table and was setting it in front of him. She looked at John in shocked surprise. There had been no grudging I-hate-asking-for-help tone in his voice. Instead, there had been what sounded like polite resignation to his limitations.

"Callie seems to have had a mellowing effect on you," Doc remarked, giving her a playful wink.

"I feel comfortable here," John admitted.

A warm glow spread over Callie. *He'd be glad to be anywhere other than the hospital,* she told herself, determined to keep a realistic perspective.

"Good food, too," Doc said, putting a slab of butter on his pancakes, then beginning to butter John's while Callie returned to the stove.

The men were finishing their second platefuls when Callie finally joined them. "There's more batter," she offered as she began to butter her own pancakes.

"It was delicious, but I can't eat another bite," John replied.

Callie noted that he'd eaten five pieces of bacon and six pancakes, and a warm glow of delight began to spread through her.

"Me either," Doc said, leaning back in his chair, a satisfied grin on his face.

It made Callie uneasy that John's appreciation of her cooking pleased her more than Doc's. I knew Doc would like it, she reasoned, again attempting to keep the reactions she was having to John Smith on an even keel. It was not only silly to care too much about what pleased him, it could also prove to be destructive.

"What do you two have planned for the day?" Doc asked.

"Callie's going to take me fishing," John replied.

"Thought we'd go over to your place and catch some of those trout you had stocked in your lake this spring," Callie elaborated.

"I asked Chester to join us, but he's busy," John interjected.

Doc almost choked on the sip of coffee he'd just taken. Managing to get it down, he stared at John. "You've met Chester?"

John frowned at the doctor. "Something wrong? He seems like a nice kid."

Doc's attention had shifted to Callie. Quickly she placed her finger on her lips to warn him not to say anything more. "No, nothing wrong with the boy, just surprised he was out so early," he replied noncommittally. Still watching her as if he wasn't certain what to think, he pushed his chair back from the table. "I've got to run. Want to check in on Helen this morning before I start my office visits." Pointedly he added, "Callie, walk me to my car. I've got some extra bandages for John."

Following him outside, Callie waited until they were out of earshot of the house, then said, "I've told you that Chester is not a figment of my imagination."

Amusement suddenly twinkled in the doctor's eyes. "I get it. You put John up to that just to see what I would say."

Callie frowned at him self-righteously. "I did not!"

The amusement left the doctor's face. "You're telling me that he actually saw Chester?"

"He can't see. He spoke to him," she corrected. "And I'm as surprised as you are. Chester usually stays away from people."

Doc shook his head. "He seems to be taking the fact that he's conversed with a ghost much better than most people would."

"That's because he doesn't know," she admitted. "I didn't exactly lie, I just sort of made him think that Chester is a normal fifteen-year-old who has the run of my place. Considering all that your Mr. Smith has been through, it didn't seem like a good idea to tell him the whole truth at this particular time."

"You're probably right," Doc agreed. He shook his head, then looked hard into her face once again. "You swear you didn't put him up to this?"

"I didn't," she replied firmly.

Again shaking his head, he reached into the car and pulled out a box of gauze. "Don't understand why, if what you're telling me is the truth, Chester hasn't shown himself to me."

"Maybe he's afraid you'll try to chase him away," she suggested.

Doc touched her cheek in a fatherly caress. "My only concern about Chester is that I don't want to see you spending your life in the company of phantoms. I want you to spend time with living people... with living, flesh and blood men. I don't want you to let your mother's mistake cheat you out of having a full and happy life."

"I don't spend time with Chester, he spends time with me, and only fleeting moments at that," she assured him. An uneasy smile played at one corner of her mouth. "As to spending time with men, you've taken care of that. I am spending time with one now."

Abruptly Doc's expression became protective. "He's behaving himself, isn't he? I thought I could trust him."

"He's behaving himself admirably," she replied.

"Good." Handing her the box of gauze, he smiled brightly. "Thanks for breakfast. See you this evening."

"Dinner will be around six."

"I'll be here," he promised, adding mischievously as he climbed into his car, "Maybe Chester will drop by."

"Maybe," Callie replied. Considering Chester's recent behavior, anything was possible. The look in Doc's eyes told her that he hadn't totally bought John's story. If the boy did show himself, Doc was in for a shock.

Back in the kitchen she found John standing in front of the sink. He was holding his coffee mug in one hand and the coffeepot in the other. Fear shook her. She'd accidentally poured hot coffee on her hand once when she was a child and had been badly burned. She started to call out but held the cry back. He was already positioning the mug against the spout and tilting the pot. If she startled him, he might lose his concentration. Standing frozen, she watched him pour the hot liquid. To her relief, he stopped well below the brim.

Setting the coffeepot aside, he used his finger to determine how full he had gotten his mug. Obviously satisfied, he turned toward her. "How'm I doing?" he asked abruptly.

Startled that he had realized she was there, Callie jumped slightly. "Just great," she replied, beginning to breathe again. Even though the danger was past, her fear remained strong and she couldn't stop herself from adding, "But you could have burned yourself badly. Really, I don't mind getting your coffee for you."

The grin on his face became a scowl. "I don't like being treated like an incompetent child."

"Obviously I haven't had quite as mellowing an effect on you as Doc thought," she muttered. Didn't he realize she was only trying to protect him? In firmer tones, she said, "I didn't mean to imply that you were incompetent. All I'm trying to do is to keep you safe and healthy until those bandages come off."

His expression grew grimmer. "My health and safety are my responsibility."

Whoever John Smith was, he had a strong stubborn streak. But he'd soon find out that she had one to match it. "You're wrong. At the moment you are my responsibility. Doc entrusted you to me and I intend to live up to his trust. Now we're going to set a few house rules. Until the bandages come off, I get to do all the pouring of any hot liquids. I also get to do all of the cooking even if you suddenly remember that you're a *cordon bleu* chef. I also do any cutting with sharp knives. If you refuse to live up to these rules, then instead of taking you fishing, I'll take you back to the hospital, and this time Doc will probably let them sedate you."

John's expression became sheepish. "I'm being unreasonable again, aren't I?"

"A bit," she replied.

He rubbed the back of his neck. "It's just that I hate this feeling of helplessness . . . of not being in control of my life."

Callie couldn't blame him. His frustration was understandable. Still, she wished he'd kept the anger between them. It would have felt safer. "How about if I carry your coffee and you go out onto the porch and sit for a while," she suggested, feeling a need to put some distance between herself and this man. "I want to clean up the kitchen, and I have a load of clothes in the washer I need to hang out. Then we can go fishing."

"In other words, you want me out from underfoot," he said with a quirky grimace. "Guess I can't blame you." The sheepishness returned. "Would you mind adding the milk to my coffee? I'm afraid I'll pour too much or add orange juice instead."

Callie shook her head. He was willing to scald himself but wanted help with the milk. Men! Aloud she said, "Sure," and after taking his cup from him, added some milk.

"Guess you might as well guide me, too," he said. "I'll hold on to your shoulder and follow a little behind."

He reached out toward her. Taking his hand, Callie placed it on her shoulder. Immediately she wished she had insisted on using his elbow to guide him. The imprint of his hand seemed almost to brand her. But that wasn't the worst.

"I apologize for being such a pain," he was saying as they began to walk through the house.

But she barely noticed his words. He was massaging her shoulder with his thumb. Obviously he wasn't even aware of what he was doing, but the action was causing her to want to purr. By the time they reached the porch, her legs were beginning to feel weak. As soon as he was seated, she handed him his coffee and hurried back inside.

"I've got to get a grip on myself," she muttered as she washed the dishes from breakfast. A flicker caught the corner of her eye. "And you," she ordered over her shoulder, "stay away from John. Explaining you to him is too difficult."

She heard a light boyish giggle then she was again alone.

"Chester seems to be very interested in the Civil War," John said as Callie drove them toward Doc's place.

Glancing toward him, she frowned. Obviously Chester had not obeyed her order.

"He talks about it as if he actually participated in it," John continued. "Sounds as if his father is a real Civil War buff, too."

"You could say his father was interested in it," she replied, recalling that according to old records, Chester's father, too, had been killed during the war.

"Was?" John questioned.

Callie frowned at herself. She'd forgotten what a good listener John was. "He died a while back."

"Losing a father at a young age can be hard on a boy," he said. Again a look of concentration creased his brow.

His silence caused Callie to glance toward him. "Did you lose your father?" she asked gently.

For a moment he didn't answer, then he shook his head. "I don't know," he replied.

A silence hung between them for the rest of the drive. Callie wanted to say something comforting but she didn't know what to say. It occurred to her that she wouldn't mind forgetting about her past and starting life anew. Then immediately she dismissed that thought. That would mean forgetting about her grandparents and Doc. Those were memories she wanted to keep.

"I brought a picnic lunch," she said as she parked by the side of Doc's house. "I want to put a few things in Doc's refrigerator, then we can walk down to the lake."

The house, set on the side of a fairly steep hill, was modern in design with an A-frame entrance. The foyer had a cathedral ceiling which produced a sense of spaciousness. On the bottom level of the house was a den, huge kitchen with a dining area, a more formal dining room, a spare bedroom, a full bathroom and a home office. On the second level was the master bedroom suite with attached bath, two other bedrooms, a guest bathroom and a huge living room. The entire back of the house was mostly windows providing a panoramic view of the surrounding wooded hills and large lake at the base of the long, sloping back lawn. A redwood deck extended out from the kitchen area and Callie decided they would have their lunch there.

Going back out to join John, she found him standing beside the car.

"Guess with all the equipment we've got to carry, it would be best if you held on to my shoulder again," she heard herself saying, wishing there was an alternative. But there wasn't. He would hate it if she insisted on making two trips so she could carry everything herself. Resignedly she handed him the tackle box, then taking his free hand, placed it on her shoulder.

It's ridiculous to be so aware of a man's touch, she chided herself as she led the way slowly toward the lake. She wasn't a child or even a teenager any longer. And why this man? Why couldn't she feel this attraction toward Tim Jekins or George O'Riely? Both had shown her attention and both were the marrying kind...safe, steady, family-type men. John Smith was a question mark. And one that will be gone in two weeks, she added.

But for the moment he was very much with her, and the feel of his hand on her shoulder matched the heat of the sun on a July afternoon. The only relief was that he wasn't massaging her this time. Forcing herself to keep a slow steady pace, she led him to a shady spot on the bank of the lake. Spreading a blanket on the dew-dampened ground, she had him sit down on it.

"Since it might be a little dangerous for both of us to let you do any fly-fishing," she said as she opened the tackle box, "we're going to bait fish." Putting some of her own special concoction of dough on his hook, she tossed his line in the water. "You hold on like this," she explained, placing the end of the rod in his hands. "Since you can't see a bobber, you'll have to keep your finger on the line. When you feel it giving little jerks then you give a little jerk back and begin reeling it in. If there's resistance, you've caught something." She had been forced to lean against him while she positioned his hands, and now her heart was beating double time. Straightening away, she took several deep breaths. Then after baiting her own line, she tossed it in and sat down on the blanket, leaving a good two feet of space between them.

The day promised to be one of those perfect spring days. The sun was warm but there was a gentle breeze to keep the air from getting too heavy. The smell of new grass and pine wafted around them. Callie tried to keep her attention focused on her bobber. When she couldn't, she let her gaze travel over the lake and to the mountainous skyline beyond. But her mind kept coming back to her companion, and she found herself watching him out of the corner of her eye. He was sitting silently, Indian fashion, holding on to the pole the way she'd instructed. But the hard set of his jaw and the way his shoulders were squared told her that he wasn't relaxed.

Suddenly he tossed his pole down between them and rose. Standing, facing the lake, he rubbed the back of his neck in an agitated fashion.

Callie, too, set her pole aside and rose with equal swiftness. "Are you all right?" she questioned, uncertain of what to say, but feeling that she needed to say something.

"Just too much time to dwell on my situation," he replied in clipped tones. "Can't even concentrate on the scenery to take my mind off wondering who I am and where I should be." Still rubbing his neck, he started to pace.

Instantly Callie raced toward him. Grabbing hold of his arm, she stopped him before he stepped over the edge of the foot-high bank and landed in the water. "This isn't the safest place to walk blindfolded," she cautioned.

His muscles tensed as he let out a low, angry, frustrated growl. "It's hard not to think of the world as being one big, flat, black land."

With every fiber of her being, Callie wished there was some way she could help him. Cupping his face in her hands, she said firmly, "In a couple of weeks you'll be able to see again. And probably by then your family will have found you. Doc made certain the police sent your picture to every missing-persons bureau in the country." Suddenly realizing she was touching him, she released him and let her hands drop down to her sides, but the sturdy feel of his jaw lingered on her palms.

He sighed harshly. "Isn't this where you offer me an ice-cream cone?"

She frowned in confusion. "What?"

Self-conscious embarrassment spread over his features. "I'm behaving like a frightened kid who got lost from his mother in a store."

"Actually you remind me more of a bear trapped in a cage," she replied, then flushed when she realized she had spoken aloud.

Grinning, he reached out toward her. Contacting her shoulders, he let his touch travel down her arms until his hands found her hands and closed around them. "I'm lucky Doc has a friend like you who's willing to take me and put up with me."

Thoroughly shaken by the trail of fire his touch had left behind, Callie's tongue came out to wet her suddenly dry lips. "You're not so difficult to put up with," she managed, glad that he could not see how disconcerted he made her. Then, afraid he might guess how much he affected her by some slip in her voice, she added dryly, "I once took care of an injured wolf pup. He not only growled but he bit."

"I promise not to bite," he assured her.

The unexpected vision of him nibbling on her ear caused a hard, hot knot to form in her abdomen, and a wave of regret that it wouldn't happen washed over her. *That's crazy,* she chided herself, but the heat of his hands still encasing hers was playing havoc with her senses. Slowly she began to free herself. "Hopefully the fish will bite," she said, determined to focus her mind on something other than him. "Are you willing to try again?"

"Provided you talk to me," he bargained, releasing her and letting her guide him back to the blanket. "You can start by describing the scenery."

As soon as Callie had him repositioned with his pole in his hands, she complied with his request.

"Sounds beautiful," he said when she finished.

Callie regarded him with a worried frown. There was a restlessness in his voice that belied the calm facade he was attempting to maintain. At any moment she expected him to toss his pole aside and try pacing into the water again. She tried to think of some interesting news item she'd seen or heard recently, but her mind was a blank. *I never was any good at small talk,* she wailed mentally.

"What do you want out of life, Callie?" he asked suddenly, breaking the silence that had fallen between them.

"I'm not sure," she answered honestly.

"You said you've never been married. Is that because you're a confirmed bachelorette or because Mr. Right hasn't come along?"

She was tempted to point out that he was getting personal again but instead she heard herself saying, "I guess I'm still looking for Mr. Right." A wistfulness entered her eyes. "In the back of my mind, I can see myself with a husband and couple of kids." She suddenly found herself picturing John in the role of her husband and two little boys who looked a lot like him playing nearby on the grass. The images shook her.

This was a very dangerous path for her thoughts to travel.

The relaxed facade vanished from his face and again a grimness came over his countenance. "I wonder if I have a couple of little kids someplace wondering where I am?" he muttered.

Probably, along with a wife he adores, Callie told herself. *And, if I'm smart I'll keep my fantasies in check and a distance between myself and him,* she added, pushing the image of the two little boys from her mind.

Again he rubbed the back of his neck in a gesture of agitation. "How could I forget everything about myself!"

"I'm sure you'll remember soon," she said encouragingly.

As much for her own welfare as for his, she silently prayed that her prediction would come true. The strength of the attraction she felt toward him scared her. The sooner he was out of her life the better.

Chapter Five

"It's ridiculous that merely touching him can cause me to feel all shaky inside," she muttered as she weeded her garden mid-morning a couple of weeks later. What made her feel even more foolish was that John's behavior over the past few days made it clear he was bored with her company.

During the first days of his stay, he'd been nearly a constant companion. Whenever she weeded, he would come out and sit in a lawn chair at the edge of the garden. Or, if she was cooking, he'd come into the kitchen and sit at the table. The second evening he was there, she'd read him the newspaper after dinner to keep him entertained. After that, this had become a regular part of their day and provided them with impersonal topics to discuss.

Also, to combat his restlessness, she'd instituted a schedule of two long walks a day. These had been the most difficult for her because she had either to hold on to his elbow or he had to hold on to her shoulder. Either way the contact was there, and no matter how hard she tried, she could not ignore the tingling of excitement it caused to spread through her.

But during the past few days, John had withdrawn from her company. Instead of coming into the kitchen while she was cooking or sitting at the edge of the garden while she was weeding, he chose to sit on the front porch or listen to the television. Yesterday he'd even cut their walk short.

"He's probably talked more to Chester than he has to me during the past two days," she muttered, then felt stupid for actually being jealous of the ghost.

The sound of a car approaching caused her muscles to tighten. Today was the day Doc was coming to take John's bandages off. She'd made John his favorite breakfast, but he'd hardly touched it and they'd barely spoken during the meal. Afterward he'd gone out onto the front porch to wait for the doctor. She'd wanted to go and sit with him, but his behavior had led her to believe that her presence wasn't welcome, so she'd opted for weeding her garden to pass the time. But now Doc was here and she was as anxious as John was to know what would happen when the bandages came off. Unable to make herself walk, she jogged to the house, pulling her gloves off as she went. She was in the kitchen washing up when Doc came in.

"I sent John into the living room," he said, joining her at the sink. As he began to wash his hands he glanced toward her. "You two have a fight?"

"No, guess he just got bored with my company," she replied with schooled nonchalance. This admission caused a jab of hurt, but she was determined not to let it show.

"Obviously he has less taste than I gave him credit for," Doc muttered. Returning his attention to washing his hands, in businesslike tones he said, "I want all the blinds in the living room closed. It'll be best if John is in a dim room when the bandages first come off. That'll give his eyes time to adjust."

"I'll take care of that right now," she replied, already on her way toward the door.

As she entered the living room, she saw John sitting stiffly in the large upholstered chair near the couch. "It's just me," she said evenly. "Doc will be here in a minute."

"I knew it was you," he replied gruffly. "I always know when it's you."

Despite the gruffness, Callie could have sworn she heard a hint of tenderness in his voice. For a moment she paused to look at him. Maybe he wasn't as bored with her company as she believed.

"Your footsteps are lighter," he added, with curt impatience.

Callie shook her head at her own stupidity. She wanted him to care, and that had caused her to read something into his voice that wasn't there. "I'm supposed to close all the blinds," she said briskly, becoming mobile and moving toward the windows.

The doctor entered as Callie finished pulling the last blind down. She wanted to stay but she didn't want to impose. "It's nearly lunchtime. I'll be in the kitchen making us something to eat if you need me," she said, heading for the door.

She saw Doc glance at John questioningly, but John said nothing as she completed her exit. In the kitchen she busied herself with making sandwiches, trying not to worry. She trusted Doc, but even he couldn't be one hundred percent certain John's sight would be completely restored.

It seemed like an eternity before the door opened. Turning she saw John. The bandage had caused him to have a strip of white that ran across his eyes, the bridge of his nose and his temples, contrasting sharply with the rest of his tanned face. But she barely noticed it as he removed the dark glasses Doc had provided him with. His eyes were brown, a dark brown like the bark of a hickory, and there was a guarded expression on his face. For a long moment, he studied her. "You're cuter than Doc said you were," he said stiffly, breaking the silence that had fallen over the room. Then, blinking as if the light was hurting his eyes, he put the glasses back on.

Callie felt confused. She should be pleased. He'd complimented her, but there had been an underlying tone in his voice that had made it sound more like an accusation.

"Doc has to get back to his office," he continued, his manner coolly businesslike, "and now that my sight has been restored, I figure it's time for me to be on my way. Doc's going to loan me some money and give me a ride into Cumberland. I just wanted to come in here and say thanks. You made the past two weeks a lot easier. Will you say goodbye to Chester for me?"

Before Callie could respond, he turned and left. *That was it? Thanks and goodbye! It's what you expected,* she reminded herself. What she hadn't expected was to feel so deserted.

"Thought I'd come in and visit while John packed his things."

Callie forced a smile as Doc came into the kitchen. "You want a glass of iced tea?" she offered, finding it suddenly very difficult to think. John was leaving. Good riddance! So why didn't she feel relieved?

"Sounds good." When she didn't move, Doc got his own glass out and poured himself some of the offered tea. Watching her worriedly, he asked, "You all right, Callie?"

Callie blinked. She'd been staring at the door as if she expected John to reappear. Glancing toward Doc, she flushed when she realized that he'd gotten his own tea. "Yeah, I'm fine. I was just wondering what I was going to do with all these sandwiches." Her gaze dropped to the table. In her nervousness she'd made enough for five people. Suddenly not wanting any reminder of John's presence in the house, she flung open a nearby drawer and pulled out the box of plastic wrap. "You men can take them with you."

She had finished wrapping the last one when a car horn sounded.

"That'll be John," Doc said, taking the bag from her. Pausing, he captured her chin in his hand. "How about having dinner with an old man tonight?"

Callie saw the concern on his face. She had hoped she wasn't being that obvious. "No, thanks. I'll be fine. Guess I just got used to having someone else around. By the time you and Mr. John Smith are on the main road, I'll be glad to have my house back to myself." A thought struck her and she smiled dryly. "At least we won't have to tell John that he spent the past couple of weeks conversing with a ghost."

He gave her an encouraging smile. "I'll give you a call later in case you change your mind."

Callie accompanied him as far as the front porch. Afraid to take a chance on allowing John to guess how much his leaving was affecting her, she didn't approach the car. Instead she waved goodbye from the porch, then went quickly back inside as the men drove off.

"I need to finish weeding," she ordered herself, trying not to think of how empty the house suddenly felt. Going out to the garden, she worked until she was dizzy from the heat. "Giving yourself sunstroke is real stupid," she berated herself, forcing herself to go back inside.

She knew what she had to do. The weeding had just been a way of trying to avoid the inevitable. Going upstairs, she entered John's room. There, she stripped the bed, then carried the bedding downstairs and shoved it into the washer. Once she had it washing, she took the spray wax and a dusting cloth and went back to his room. She would erase any signs that he had ever been in her house, and in the process she would put him out of her mind.

"He couldn't wait to get out of here," she reminded herself curtly as she dusted the chest of drawers. In fairness she added, "Of course, it was only natural for him to want to go in search of himself. He had nothing to hold him here.''

By the time she had finished with the dusting and was doing the vacuuming, she was telling herself that by tomorrow she would have him totally out of her mind. Then she opened the closet door. Her grandfather's robe was hanging there. A faint lingering scent of John's after-shave reached her nostrils, and her stomach knotted. As if she'd discovered a snake poised to strike, she slammed the door closed.

Her legs felt shaky. She raised her foot and pressed the button to turn off the vacuum. Furious with herself she grabbed the machine, carried it into the hall and shoved it into its storage space in the hall closet. Stalking downstairs, she unloaded the washer, hung the bedding out to dry, then returned to John's room. ''This is not John Smith's room,'' she corrected her thoughts as she grabbed the robe out of the closet. ''This is my spare room.''

Carrying the robe downstairs, she dropped it into the washer. ''And that's the end of Mr. John Smith,'' she told herself as she added soap and began the cycle.

But that evening, as she sat in the living room holding the newspaper unread in her hands, she found herself glancing toward the place on the couch where he had sat. Suddenly Chester was there, standing in front of the couch and looking at John's spot, too. ''It's stupid for us to miss him,'' she informed the ghost with a scowl. ''He couldn't wait to leave.''

Chester's image flickered and then was gone. Callie drew a tired breath. It wasn't fair of her to be angry. "I do hope he finds himself," she said with quiet sincerity.

During the next few days Callie kept busy. She did the spring cleaning she'd been putting off for the past year, and her garden was probably the best weeded in the county. But nothing could ease the sense of aloneness that persisted within her.

"I've got to shake this," she ordered herself. It was evening and John had been gone a full week. In an effort to combat the restlessness that filled her, she had the television on and was trying to force herself to read the evening paper. Neither was helping. Tossing the paper aside, she rose and began to pace. "Now I'm even behaving like John," she muttered to herself grudgingly. "What I need is to get out and see more people."

As if in response to her words, the phone rang. It was George O'Riely. Callie had heard that he and Sally James had had an argument and split up. Apparently it was true, because he'd called to ask Callie for a date.

"Sure," she agreed. George was pleasant company, and hadn't she just been telling herself that she needed to get out? After arranging for him to pick her up around six-thirty the next evening, she hung up.

Suddenly a loud clap of thunder shook the house. "Looks like we're in for a real blow," Callie informed her image in the mirror. A second, even louder, clap sounded as she hurried through the house closing the windows. Outside the gray dusk had turned black. She saw a streak of lightning flash straight downward and the cracking sound that followed told her that it had hit a tree. Suddenly, huge raindrops began to pelt the window she had just closed. Spring thunderstorms were always the worst.

"Candles," she ordered herself. A storm like this could easily knock out the electricity. Heading toward the kitchen, she was stopped short by a knocking on her front door.

"Who in the world would be out in this storm?" she muttered to herself. "Doc," she answered as she hurried to open it. But it wasn't the doctor. Every muscle in her body tensed at the sight of John Smith standing there.

"Mind if I come in?" he asked gruffly.

The rain was blowing onto the porch and already his shirt and jeans were beginning to get wet. "Sure, come on in," she managed, stepping aside to allow him to enter. He was back. She hadn't expected to ever see him again but there he was. He looked tired and thinner than when he'd left, and she saw him shiver.

"Rain's cold," he said.

"The storm came in from the north," she replied, watching him, wondering why he'd come back and hoping she had something to do with it.

"Sorry to bother you," he apologized.

"I went by Doc's place but he was out. I thought he might be here."

He was only looking for Doc. Fool, she chided herself. But her disappointment was quickly overshadowed by her concern for him. "Are you ill?"

"No, just looking for a place to stay for a while," he replied.

The offer to let him stay with her made it all the way to the tip of her tongue. Shocked, she held it back. How could she even consider issuing an open invitation like that? How long was *a while?* She couldn't have a virile stranger staying with her—especially not this one. Her reactions toward him were much too strong. Who knew where they might lead? Her jaw tensed. She wouldn't make the same mistake her mother had made. Seeing him shiver again, she realized that the storm was cooling the house. "Come on into the living room. I'll build a fire."

But instead of following her, he hesitated. "Mind if I use your phone to call Doc's service and leave a message for him?"

Glancing back toward him, she caught a glimpse of uneasiness in his features before his expression became shuttered. Obviously he didn't want her getting even the slightest notion he'd come back because of her. "Sounds like a good idea to me," she replied, then continued on toward the living room.

He entered just as she finished building a pyramid of crumpled balls of paper and kindling. "The service couldn't give me any idea when Doc would call back. As soon as the storm blows over, I'll just walk over to his place. He's bound to show up sooner or later."

He couldn't wait to get away from her. Just like the day he left, she reminded herself. Acidly she wondered why he'd even come knocking on her door. I suppose any port would do in a storm like this one, she decided as another loud clap of thunder caused the windows to rattle. Well, if he wanted to get away, she'd help. The sooner he was gone, the better. "I've got a key to Doc's place. I'll drive you over as soon as the rain lets up. He won't mind."

"Thanks."

The relief in his voice needled her. Turning her attention back to building the fire, she struck a match and lighted the pyramid. She knew it was cowardly, but she didn't want to face him. It hurt that he found her company so unsatisfactory. *I suppose I'm a strong reminder of a very difficult time in his life,* she reasoned. *And several embarrassing moments,* she added, recalling his reaction when he'd discovered her waiting outside the bathroom that first night. Continuing to watch the fire as if it required her full attention to get started, she asked with forced casualness, "What have you been doing this past week?"

"I went to Baltimore and to Washington, D.C., and checked with the police there. They had my picture on file but no one had made any inquiries," he replied with a strong edge of impatience.

Callie heard the couch creak and knew he had sat down in his old spot.

"Doc had loaned me some money, and I found jobs as a dishwasher to supplement it." Dryly he added, "Now I know what they mean when they talk about dishpan hands."

Callie glanced over her shoulder toward him. He looked as if he belonged there on her couch. But he doesn't, she corrected, forcing the thought from her mind. Again she returned her attention to the fireplace. The kindling had caught and she began to build up the fire with heavier logs.

"Then yesterday I was at the bus station ready to purchase a ticket to New York, when it occurred to me that maybe I was chasing shadows," he continued, a tiredness entering his voice. "I have no idea where I'm from. I could be searching in the wrong direction. Besides, if anyone came looking for me, they'd contact the police here. That's the address on my missing person's file. That was when I realized that I might as well come back here. If I never get my memory back, I can't think of anyplace that would be any better to start a new life. Doc had offered to put me up for a while, so I decided to accept his offer until I can find a job and a place of my own."

He'd come back to stay, but only because he had no place better to go. The fire was blazing now. She'd seem like an idiot if she kept staring at it. Rising, she turned to face him. He looked even more tired than he had in the hall. That she cared irritated her. He had no feelings for her. Still she heard herself asking, "Have you had any dinner?"

He shook his head. "But I don't want to be a bother."

"It's not a bother to fix you a sandwich," she replied, glad of any excuse to escape.

Once in the kitchen, she made him a cup of hot chocolate to go with the roast beef sandwich. She told herself it was only because he needed it to ward off the chill of the storm and not because she remembered how much he had liked her hot chocolate. Returning to the living room, she discovered him staring into the fire, his jaw tense and his expression grim.

His features became guarded when he noticed her approaching, and he accepted the food with a polite "Thank you."

He ate hungrily and she wondered when he'd last had a decent meal. It's only natural to be concerned about one's fellow man, she told herself, furious with how much she cared. Again the need to escape was strong. "I'll make you another sandwich," she said, already moving toward the door.

He made no move to stop her, and this time she also brought him a large slice of apple pie.

"You're as good a cook as I remembered," he said when he had finished the second sandwich and the pie.

Again she heard the hint of an accusation in his voice and frowned. "Usually people are happy to be served food by a good cook," she remarked curtly, confused and hurt by his manner.

Rubbing the back of his neck, he grimaced apologetically. "I'm sorry. I meant that as a compliment. I'm just real tired."

Callie's nerves felt like little needles pricking her. It was obvious that he didn't want to be there, and she'd had about as much of Mr. Smith's company as she could take. The storm was still blowing outside, but she was going to offer to drive him to Doc's place anyway. Then her front door opened and footsteps sounded in the hall.

In the next moment Doc appeared in the doorway of the living room. He paused there for a moment as if uncertain of his reception. His gaze traveled from John to Callie, then back to John. Becoming mobile again, he continued into the room. "So you came back," he said, approaching John.

Callie was surprised to see that the welcoming smile on Doc's face didn't reach his eyes. They weren't hostile but there seemed to be a question in them. She'd thought he had liked John Smith and would be pleased to see him.

"Don't know if it was such a good idea," John replied as he accepted the doctor's handshake.

The doc's smile warmed to one of fatherly concern. "It's always good to be among friends."

"Yeah," John replied.

Friend, Callie corrected mentally. John Smith considered Doc a friend, but he obviously didn't put her in that category. "I was just about to drive Mr. Smith over to your place." Pride suddenly caused her to add, "I have a date tomorrow night and I want to get my beauty rest."

"Heard George O'Riely and Sally James have broken up," Doc said watching her for confirmation that he'd made the right guess as to whom she had a date with.

"That seems to be the case," she replied.

Doc frowned worriedly. "It's always smart to be cautious about a relationship when one of the people involved is on the rebound."

Callie flushed. She was used to the doctor playing the role of protective father, but not in front of John Smith. "I can take care of myself, Doc. I've been doing it for years," she returned pointedly.

Nodding, he put an arm around her shoulders and gave her a hug. "I know. But you're as close to a daughter as I have. I just don't want to see you getting hurt."

A shadow passed across Callie's eyes. "You don't have to worry about me. I don't have any illusions where men are concerned." A prickling on the side of her neck caused her to glance toward John. He was studying her, his gaze shuttered. He's probably thinking that only a man on the rebound would be interested in someone as dull as me, she mused. Suddenly she wanted him out of her house. "It sounds as if the rain has let up. You two better get going. There might be a second storm on the way."

Doc glanced toward John. "Could be," he agreed.

Callie had the impression that Doc's words carried some sort of second meaning. But if they did, John was refusing to rise to the bait. He turned toward Callie, his expression one of formal politeness. "Thanks for the shelter and the food." Then picking up his duffel bag, he started toward the door.

"I'll see you on Sunday," Doc said, causing Callie to remember she was fixing a Sunday dinner for him. "Around two all right?"

She nodded. Politeness forced her to add, "You might as well ask John if he wants to join us since he's staying with you." The thought of sitting at a table with Mr. John Smith wasn't something she was looking forward to, but she doubted he'd accept the invitation, anyway. The front door opened, confirming her belief that he couldn't get out of her house fast enough to suit him.

Doc frowned at the empty doorway through which John had so recently exited. "Don't know if that's such a good idea," he muttered.

So John's quick departure had not been lost on Doc. How could it have been? He'd practically run from the room. "Maybe not. Forget I mentioned it."

Doc turned back toward her and placed an arm around her shoulders. "Besides, I could use some private time with you to give you some fatherly advice about love and marriage and getting involved with men on the rebound."

"I'm not going to get involved," she assured him again as she walked with him to the front door.

John was already in the car. *No doubt I won't be seeing him at my door again,* she thought as she watched the car disappearing down the drive. "It's just as well," she added, her shoulders straightening. "I don't know how I could have cared so much about him. He can barely stand to be around me." Maybe it was just as well that he had come back. As hard as she'd tried, she hadn't been able to put him entirely out of her mind. There had even been moments of obvious insanity during the past week when she'd suddenly found herself missing him. But her encounter with him that night was certain to be a cure.

Carrying his empty plate and glass into the kitchen, she then washed them. "If I never see him again, I'll die happy," she announced to the room as she dried the dishes and put them away.

Chapter Six

"Good afternoon."

Every muscle in Callie's back tensed. She had to be imagining that voice. Her grip on the ladder tightened and she glanced down. It hadn't been her imagination. It *was* John. She'd been certain after his quick departure the night before that he wouldn't come around again.

"If you're looking for Doc, he's not here," she said, returning her attention to scraping the paint off the side of the house. She'd been tense this morning. She'd told herself it had nothing to do with Mr. John Smith's return, but her nerves had remained on edge. Finally she'd decided that this was as good a time as any to begin the major project of repainting her house. It was getting close to mid-afternoon now and she'd been standing on this ladder for hours. At noon she'd taken a short break but quickly returned to her work.

Her arms and legs ached, and she was in no mood to be polite to a man who obviously couldn't stand her company.

"I wasn't looking for Doc," he replied evenly.

Again she looked down at him. "I can't believe you're here to see me," she said dryly. "I got the impression you couldn't get away from me fast enough." *Damn!* she cursed herself. *Why had she said that? It sounded as if she cared what he thought of her.*

He shifted uneasily, then met her gaze levelly, his features shuttered. "I remembered you telling me that you were going to have to repaint your house this summer. Thought I would come over and help as a sort of thank-you for all you did for me when I was blinded."

Callie scowled down at him. He didn't want to be there. "You've already thanked me, that's enough."

His jaw hardened, and he frowned. "You shouldn't be climbing around on a ladder when there's no one else around. What if you fall? You could lie there for hours or days before someone found you."

Now he was giving her advice! "I'm quite capable of looking after myself, Mr. Smith."

Shoving his hands into the pockets of his jeans, he again shifted uneasily. "I didn't mean to imply you weren't," he said gruffly. His shoulders straightened. "But I've come to help you paint this house, and I intend to do just that."

Callie's scowl deepened. He was only here because he felt he owed her a debt, and she didn't want help from someone who could barely stand to be around her. "Shouldn't you be out looking for a job?"

"I've already found one. Doc got a call this morning and I went with him. Seems Jacob Kelps was working on adding a new addition to his barn when he fell and broke his leg. I'm going to finish the job under his supervision. Doc's got him pretty doped up today for the pain, so I can't start until tomorrow. It doesn't pay much, but it beats doing dishes."

Callie studied him narrowly. There was a glint of enthusiasm in his eyes. She wondered how long that would last. Jacob was one of the older members of their community. A widower with one daughter, he'd worked long, hard hours all of his life to make his farm prosper. He demanded the same of anyone he hired, and that meant ten-hour work days in the summer when it stayed light longer. As a result he found it difficult to find anyone who would work for him. "If I were you, I'd spend today resting," she advised, again returning her attention to scraping paint.

"I've come to help. You shouldn't be here alone climbing around on ladders."

The reprimanding edge in his voice was the last straw. He didn't even like her. It took a lot of nerve for him to think he could tell her what she should and shouldn't do! Climbing down from the ladder, she faced him. "Go away, Mr. Smith. I don't need your help and I don't want your advice."

He raked a hand agitatedly through his hair. His jaw tensed and Callie had the impression he was going to argue with her. Then abruptly he turned and began to walk away. But before he had gone two paces, he stopped and pivoted around to face her again. "You could hire Chester to help you. I'll pay him."

Callie glared at him. It was as if he was determined to appoint himself her guardian. "That's ridiculous. I know Jacob, and he's not going to be paying you so much that you have money to spare."

"I'll be able to handle it," he replied in a low growl. "Besides, it will be good for Chester to have something productive to do with his time."

"For a man who can't even remember how he's spent his life, you certainly seem to have a lot of opinions about how others should spend their lives," she snapped. Immediately she regretted having thrown his loss of memory at him but her nerves were brittle. He didn't want to be in her life, but he wanted to tell her how to live it. "Sorry," she apologized stiffly. "I shouldn't have said anything about your memory. That was a low blow."

He shifted uneasily. "Guess I deserved it," he replied gruffly. "But what about hiring Chester? It's not such a bad idea."

Callie drew a shaky breath as she found herself wishing that his persistence was due to an honest concern for her. But it wasn't. It was merely a debt he felt he needed to repay. She desperately wanted him to leave. Telling him the truth about Chester should do the trick, she decided. Squaring her shoulders, she faced him evenly. "No one can hire Chester. He's a ghost."

John stared at her in disbelief. "He's a *what?*"

"A ghost, an apparition, a spirit," she replied.

He shook his head. "You're joking."

"No, I'm not," she assured him.

Rubbing the back of his neck, he regarded her in silence for a long moment, then said incredulously, "Ghost? You're telling me that I conversed with a ghost?"

Callie nodded. "That's about it." He looked so disconcerted, she almost wished she hadn't told him. But if it would get rid of him, it was worth it.

His gaze narrowed on her. "What about Doc? Has he ever seen or talked to Chester?"

"No. Other than my grandmother and myself, you're the only other person I know of who Chester has seen fit to communicate with," she replied honestly.

His mouth formed a straight, hard line. "What's Doc think about Chester?"

Callie shrugged. "He used to think Chester was a figment of mine and my grandmother's imagination. Now I don't know."

Accusation entered his eyes. "You could have warned me. He probably thinks I'm operating with one brick short of a load."

His anger raised her ire and she glared at him with self-righteous indignation. "When your eyes were bandaged, I thought it would be too much of a shock in your condition. You already had enough on your mind. After you got your eyesight back, you raced out of here so fast I didn't even have time to say goodbye. Besides, I didn't figure we'd ever see you again, anyway."

Shoving his hands into the pockets of his jeans, John paced away from her, then turned and paced back until he was barely two feet from her. Glowering down at her, he asked curtly, "Is Chester here now?"

Callie let her gaze travel slowly over their surroundings. His coldness toward her had hurt, and she now found herself feeling amused by his chagrin. *That's mean of you,* she berated herself, as her gaze returned to him. With an indifferent shrug, she said, "I don't see him." She had meant to stop there but an impish urge caused her to add dryly, "Do you?"

John glanced around them. "No," he growled. Suddenly one corner of his mouth tilted into a dry, cynical smile. "But I think I'll just stick around and help you paint your house. If this Chester is really a ghost, sooner or later he's bound to show himself again, and I'd like a look at the apparition I spent time talking to."

Callie stared at him in shock. She'd been certain the mention of Chester would send him running. "I don't want you here," she snapped. "You're only here because you feel you have a debt to pay. Well, consider it paid. Now go away!"

He raised an eyebrow in a challenging fashion. "Are you afraid I'll discover you haven't been honest about Chester? Maybe you hired some kid to come over and play the part to make Doc a believer. After all, I was the perfect patsy. I didn't know anyone around here, so I wouldn't recognize the voice, and I was blind so I can't contest your word."

"I would never do such a thing!" Callie growled, stunned that he would make such an accusation.

"Probably not," he agreed, his smile returning. "But I'll just stick around and see for myself."

Callie knew defeat when she saw it. "Fine, if you insist," she conceded, as a solution dawned on her. "You can work on the west side of the house. There's another ladder in the garage and a scraper on the back porch." At least that way she wouldn't have to see him. She could even forget he was there, she told herself, as he started around the house.

But out of sight didn't put him out of her mind. Besides, he didn't stay out of sight. About half an hour later, he came around the house carrying a glass of ice water.

"I brought you a drink," he called up to her. "You have to be careful and not get dehydrated in weather like this."

The day was a scorcher. Summer had come full force and the temperature was in the nineties, but she didn't need or want him telling her how to take care of herself. "I've got a jug up here with me," she informed him haughtily, motioning to the jug she had fastened to her ladder.

"You should still take a break once in a while," he called back.

She knew he was right but it irked her to admit it. *You're being childish,* she warned herself. But that didn't stop her from saying, "I'll take a break when I'm ready to take a break."

"Suit yourself," he muttered and went back around the house.

"Ouch! Darn!" she cursed as she climbed out of her shower a few hours later. Around five she had quit to give herself plenty of time to prepare for her date.

She'd gone around to the west side of the house and found John busily working. After informing him that it was time to stop for the day, she'd gone inside to bathe. The moment the warm water hit the back of her neck and her legs, she knew she'd been an idiot. She'd bound her hair up in a ponytail, which offered no protection for her neck against the sun, and she'd worn shorts. On top of that she hadn't been able to find any suntan lotion that morning to rub on, and she'd been too tense to care. Now both her neck and legs were sunburned. The worst was the sensitive skin behind the knees.

"Doc is going to scream at me for being so stupid," she muttered, standing in front of her mirror looking over her shoulder at the reflection of the scarlet backs of her legs. She bent her knee, and the pain caused her to wince.

Breathing a disgruntled sigh, she found a tube of ointment and gently applied it to the burned portions of her anatomy. "Now I feel like a greased pig," she informed the image in the mirror.

The thought of putting on panty hose caused her to cringe. She stared at the sundress hanging in her closet. She could wear it bare-legged. But as she pulled on a pair of panties, tears came to her eyes when she was forced to bend her legs. She couldn't possibly sit through a dinner and a movie in this condition. Besides, she'd get ointment all over everything she sat on, including the upholstery of George's car. The date was going to have to be canceled. Sitting down on the bed, she grimaced as her knees again bent, creasing the sunburned skin. Quickly she dialed George's number.

There was no answer. She glanced at the clock. It was only a quarter to six. Surely he wasn't on his way to her house yet. She'd wait a few minutes, then dial again. Gently she eased herself onto the bed, then flipped over onto her stomach.

"Stupid, stupid, stupid," she cursed into her pillow. Then breathing another disgruntled sigh, she lay silent.

That was when she first noticed it . . . the sound of scraping. Gritting her teeth, she rose from the bed, found a robe, then went over to her window and peered out. John was standing on the ground below, still working on preparing the wood for painting. "I thought I told you it was time to quit," she called down to him, wanting to get rid of him before he found out about her sunburn. She felt like enough of a fool without having him to confirm it.

"You have a date. I don't, and there's still a lot of light left," he called back, continuing to scrape.

"I'm getting a headache from hearing you scraping," she lied. "Now will you please stop and go home."

He frowned up at her. "If you insist."

She drew a relieved breath as he picked up the ladder lying on the grass and began carrying it toward the garage. "One down and one to go," she muttered as she moved back toward the phone on the table beside her bed. But again she got no answer at George's home.

For the next fifteen minutes she lay stretched out on her bed, then, bowing to the inevitable, she found a bra and put it on. From her closet she took out a loose-fitting, lightweight cotton dress and pulled it on. She had to meet George and apologize for not being able to keep their date. She didn't bother with shoes.

Just walking down the stairs was painful. At least John was gone, she told herself, trying to find a bright side. But as she stepped out onto the front porch, she came to an abrupt halt. John wasn't gone. He was there, sitting in the chair he'd always used, with his feet propped up on the rail.

"Hope you don't mind. Thought I'd take a little rest and cool off before I started walking back to Doc's place." As he spoke his gaze traveled over her. "Rather casual for a date," he said, his attention coming to rest on her bare feet. "Or is that the new style and it's one of the things I can't remember?"

Anger masked Callie's embarrassment. "No, it's not a new style. I've decided to cancel my date." He raised a questioning eyebrow, and she felt compelled to give him a reason. "I've got a headache," she lied, then comforted herself by noting that she was developing one. Curtly she added, "Now will you please leave?"

"Looks like you forgot to tell George," he said, lazily lifting his legs down and then standing, as a car turned into the drive and made its way toward the house.

"He wasn't home when I tried to call," she replied. She was going to tell George the truth about the sunburn but she didn't want to do that in front of John. "The polite thing for you to do would be to leave," she added pointedly.

"I know my memory's a bit foggy but I could swear that the polite thing to do at this point would be to wait for an introduction," he contended as George parked.

There was no time to argue. George had left his car and was walking toward them, carrying a bouquet of flowers. "You'll get your introduction, and then I want you to leave," she ordered in a low growl.

"Sure thing," he replied dryly. "Just trying to be polite."

Polite would have been for him to leave when she'd told him to half an hour ago, but there wasn't time to point this out. Turning her attention to George, she greeted him with a welcoming smile. He was a large man, three inches over six feet tall and weighing around two hundred pounds. But none of the weight was fat. It was all muscle built from years of working with horses. George bred, raised and trained some of the finest quarter horses in the state. His sun-bleached blond hair, cut in a conservative style, contrasted markedly with his tanned skin as did his pale blue eyes. He wasn't exactly handsome but he was pleasant to look at and his easy-going manner made him a comfortable companion.

"Always did like barefooted women," George said good-naturedly, giving Callie an approving wink as he climbed the steps to the porch. In an easy drawl he added, "But most restaurants require shoes."

"I'm going to have to cancel our date," she replied apologetically. "I tried to call, but you'd already left."

"I went by to pick these up." The good-naturedness left his face to be replaced by a cynical scowl. "You might as well have them." As he thrust them toward her, his gaze swung to John and then back to her. "Looks like a better offer came along. I never thought that was like you, Callie."

"It isn't." It was clear his feelings were hurt. Normally she would never have expected George to make such an accusation. Obviously his breaking up with Sally had left him a bit on the distrustful side where women were concerned. Because John was still there, she'd been considering pleading a headache but she couldn't do that now. George would never believe it and she didn't want to alienate him. "I did something real stupid today. I was scraping paint, standing on a ladder and got the back of my legs sunburned." Turning, she lifted her skirt just above the knee joint to give proof to her words. "I don't want to get ointment all over your upholstery. Besides, bending them to sit properly hurts like the dickens. I wouldn't be good company."

George let out a low whistle and shook his head sympathetically. "Thought you were smarter than that."

John regarded her grimly. "I thought you were, too," he muttered. Then, turning his attention to George, he held out his hand. "My name's John Smith."

"I figured that was who you were," George replied, his gaze traveling speculatively over the other man. "I heard you were back in town."

John's attention returned to Callie. "I came by to help Callie with the scraping, but I was working on the other side of the house. I didn't notice she wasn't properly attired."

The censure in his voice caused the hairs on the back of Callie's neck to rise. The urge was strong to tell him that her attire was none of his business, but because of George's presence, she held back the comment.

"My name's George O'Riely," George said, accepting the offered handshake. His anger now entirely gone, he smiled with friendly interest. "I also heard you're going to work for Jacob for a while."

John nodded and returned the man's smile. "I don't know if I'm skilled at anything, so I thought I'd better take what came along."

"I'll be needing some help come harvest time. Got to put in feed to keep my horses fed over the winter. If you're still around, look me up," George offered.

Callie stood feeling forgotten. Apparently men find my presence easy to ignore, she mused acidly. "If you two will excuse me, I'll be going back inside," she cut in dryly. Remembering her manners, she forced herself to give George a smile and added in more pleasant tones, "Thanks for the flowers. I'm sorry about having to break the date."

He grinned at her. "Tell you what. The Fourth of July Picnic's next week. By that time your sunburn should be better. You could go with me to it."

She told herself it shouldn't matter, but it pleased her that George was asking her for a new date in front of John. "Sure," she replied, flashing him her brightest smile. "That sounds like fun." Out of the corner of her eye, she caught a look of disgruntlement on John's face just before his expression became shuttered. He probably can't understand why George would want to spend any time with me, she thought as she gave him a haughty glance then went inside. Well, what John Smith thought was of no interest to her.

She was in the kitchen fixing herself a glass of iced tea and a sandwich when she heard a car leaving. Finally she was alone. Breathing a sigh of relief, she picked up her dinner and started toward the living room. But as she left the kitchen, the sound of a man's voice brought her to an abrupt halt.

"Doc, I'm over at Callie's place and I think you should come over here and take a look at her. She's got herself seriously sunburned," John was saying in an angry, impatient voice.

He was interfering in her life again! But what really irked her was the implication in his tone that she was not capable of taking care of herself. Callie strode out into the hall as he hung up the phone. "There was no reason for you to call Doc," she snapped.

"Looks to me like you burned yourself badly enough to blister," he retorted, his manner suggesting that he was still finding it difficult to believe anyone could be so careless. "I thought it would be wise to have him take a look. He might have a stronger ointment than the one you used."

Pride caused her shoulders to straighten. "If I blister, it's my business, not yours," she returned. "And the ointment I used will work just fine." He was watching her with that closed expression on his face as if he found her impossible to deal with. Well, she hadn't asked for his help. He was the one who had butted uninvited back into her life. She was uncomfortable and tired. Her temper took control. "You've made it clear that you don't really want to be here, and I don't want you here. If you honestly cared about my well-being it would be different. But as it is, I find your self-appointed guardianship intolerable. Now get out of my house and stay out!"

His jaw tensed. "Maybe I have been a little overbearing." His gaze narrowed on her as he reached out and touched her cheek gently. "But you're wrong about one thing. I *do* care about you. I don't want anything bad or unhappy to ever happen to you."

His fingers left a trail of fire. But it was the warmth in his eyes that truly shook her. There was a protectiveness in those dark depths that caused her toes to want to curl. He *did* care. She chewed on her bottom lip in confusion.

Suddenly the guardedness returned to his gaze. "You and Doc are the closest to family that I have right now," he finished gruffly, drawing his hand back.

His words stung. He cared about her in a way he would care for a sister . . . an *incompetent* sister. Pride refused to allow her to let her hurt show. She took a deep breath as she regained control. "Then I appreciate your concern," she said levelly. "But it really isn't necessary."

He raised a cynical eyebrow as if to question this last statement as his gaze traveled to her legs. But the sound of an approaching car interrupted any comment he might have been considering making. "Doc's here," he announced. "No sense in not letting him take a look at you," he added, moving toward the door.

"I'll be in the living room," Callie informed his retreating back. There was no sense in arguing with him. He was obviously determined to have his way. Resignedly she went into the living room. Plopping herself down in a chair, she stifled a scream of pain and cursed at herself for forgetting about her sunburn. Only John Smith and his meddling could have caused her to put something so painful out of her mind. Moving cautiously, she lifted her feet and let her heels rest on the coffee table, stretching her legs out straight. She didn't want John Smith as a surrogate brother. It had been easier when she thought he didn't care at all. Now how could she order him out of her life?

"Heard you got a little sun."

She looked up to see Doc entering. Glancing past him she expected to see John also, but he wasn't there.

"John's waiting for me on the porch," he said as if he could read her mind.

Callie frowned self-consciously. Of course John was waiting on the porch. He didn't care about her in a way that would cause him to hover over her like a guardian angel. He was more of the thorn-in-the-side kind of self-appointed watchman who showed up to call attention to her defects. "He shouldn't have phoned you in the first place," she grumbled.

Doc was already kneeling beside her, examining her legs. "Thought you had better sense than this," he said, shaking his head.

"I just wasn't thinking too straight," she replied, her frown deepening as her gaze again traveled toward the door.

Following her line of vision, Doc frowned worriedly. "Maybe I'd better have a talk with John. It might be best if he stayed away."

Callie flushed. She certainly didn't want John to guess he'd had such a distracting effect on her. "I wouldn't want him to get the idea that this was his fault," she said stiffly. "It was my own stupidity."

For a moment Doc looked as if he was going to argue with her, then he shrugged. "Guess the two of you will have to work out whatever there is between you sometime, anyway."

The way he'd said it made it sound as if he suspected a romantic involvement, and considering John's behavior, he had to assume it was only one-sided. Pride refused to allow her to leave him with the impression she was suffering from a teenage crush on a man who had no interest in her. "There is nothing 'between' us," she informed him brusquely. "Our only problem is that he thinks of me as a kid sister and I don't want a big brother. I'm used to being on my own. And," she added pointedly, "I like it that way."

For a long moment Doc regarded her in a grim silence, then he rose. "Just keep using what you're using and take better care next time," he ordered.

"I will," she assured him, relieved that he had dropped the subject of her and John Smith.

She remained in the living room when he left. Getting up and down was too painful. When she heard the sound of his car driving away, she knew that this time she was alone.

A flicker in the corner caught her eye and the faint image of a young boy began to appear. "The next time Mr. John Smith is here, I'd appreciate it if you'd make an appearance. Maybe that will satisfy him, and he'll go away and leave me alone," she suggested tersely.

An impish grin spread over Chester's face, then as quickly as he had appeared, he vanished.

Chapter Seven

The Fourth of July dawned clear and hot. Callie hadn't seen a great deal of Doc or John since the day she had gotten sunburned. Doc had even had to cancel out on Sunday dinner because of an emergency at the hospital, and because Jacob wanted his barn finished while the weather was clear, John had worked every day—including the past Saturday and Sunday.

The hard work seemed to suit him. He was already looking stronger and healthier. On Sunday, she'd heard Jacob talking about him at church to some of the other men. "Never had a better worker," he'd said. "Never complains, though he did curse a bit when he hit his thumb with the hammer. I told him to take time off and come to church this morning, but he said he was afraid the weather was going to change. I suspect he'll have the roof on by the time I get home."

Callie had suddenly had a vision of John on the roof of the barn. What if he fell? The thought had sent a cold chill through her. There would be no one there to help him. All during the sermon she'd worried. *It's my duty to worry,* she'd reasoned when she couldn't put the thought of him out of her mind. He'd appointed himself her guardian, and in a way that made her feel a responsibility to him. *And responsibility is all I feel,* she'd told herself firmly.

Although John hadn't taken time off to go to church, he had taken time off to go and get a driver's license, and Doc had lent him an old car to get around with. Each day one of the two men had dropped by in the evening on their way home to check on her, but neither had stayed long. In John's case, this suited her just fine. But it bothered her that Doc wasn't spending as much time as he used to. It wasn't his choice, though.

"Been one heck of a rash of accidents this summer," he'd complained Monday evening when he'd come by.

"You look tired," she'd said sympathetically. "You should have gone straight home to bed."

"Tonight was my night to check on you. I wouldn't want you falling off that ladder and no one finding you for a couple of days," he'd replied.

Callie frowned as she recalled the conversation. She didn't mind Doc keeping an eye on her. It was, in fact, comforting to know there was someone in her life who cared enough about her welfare to take the time to drop by. But John's concern grated on her nerves. She sensed a growing discomfort in him when he was around her as if he'd been reconsidering his earlier declaration and wasn't quite sure he honestly wanted to count her as an adopted sister. As the days passed it became more and more clear to her that it was a sense of duty and nothing more that brought him there. She hated being thought of as an obligation.

She shrugged her shoulders as if that could shake off thoughts of the man. She had a date for the picnic and she was going to have a good time. The Fourth of July was always a big day in Winklersville. Nearly the whole town gathered at the park. For the past three years, she'd gone with Doc and provided their picnic lunch. Since she was going with George this year, she had volunteered to pack Doc and John a basket of their own, and Doc had accepted.

For both baskets, she'd made fried chicken and homemade bread. For Doc and John she'd also made an apple pie. That this was John's favorite dessert she chose to ignore, telling herself that since Doc didn't care what dessert was in the basket, she might as well make something one of them would appreciate. As for George, she called him to find out what he especially liked, and as a result she'd baked a chocolate cake. After all, he was her date and she wanted him to feel special.

She had finished dressing for her date when she heard a car pulling up. Pausing in front of her mirror she made a final quick inspection. Her reactions to John had convinced her that it was time she seriously started looking around for a husband. Thus, she'd worked hard to look her best today. She wasn't so certain George was the answer to her prayers but there would be other eligible males around. Her hand went up to her hair. Its dark, wavy tresses were loosely gathered back from her face with narrow pink-and-white ribbons wound together to form a decorative band. The ends of the ribbons dangled down her back in a festive array. Her sundress was a lightweight white cotton with pink flowers that matched the ribbons. She'd gone out and bought it especially for the picnic. It was an off-the-shoulders affair with spaghetti straps, a fitted bodice and a full skirt. Admittedly it was a little more daring than her usual style. But she'd decided that a little change wouldn't do any harm. On her feet she wore a pair of white sandals. The only drawback was that she hadn't been able to wear hose because of her sunburn. It had begun to peel and itched too much when she tried to pull on the full-length stockings, so she'd had to settle for bare legs.

The car had stopped and she went downstairs to greet her visitor. She'd expected either the Doc or George. Instead it was John. "Doc asked me to pick up the basket. He got an emergency call and will meet me at the picnic," he explained as he entered and followed her into the kitchen.

Callie felt the muscles in her back tighten. That was another thing she'd noticed lately—he always offered an excuse for being at her home, as if to say that given his choice, he wouldn't be there. She had the most tremendous urge to take the apple pie out of the basket and throw it at him. Instead she nodded toward the table and said with dismissal, "The basket nearest you is yours and Doc's, and the yellow jug has lemonade in it. Have a good time." She expected him to grab the basket and jug and make a quick exit, but instead he lingered near the door.

"You look real nice," he said stiffly, breaking the silence between them.

A surge of pleasure rushed through her. But when she turned back toward him and saw the guarded expression on his face, the pleasure disappeared. He was merely being polite. "Thanks," she returned and started toward the door. She was in no mood to make small talk with a man who considered it his duty to be nice to her.

"How is your sunburn?" he asked, picking up the basket and jug, then following her.

She breathed a resigned sigh. Here comes the speech, she thought. She'd been expecting it. Actually it was a little late in coming. She'd been certain she would hear it the first night he'd come by to check on her, but he'd barely said two words. He'd merely assured himself that she was finished climbing on the ladder for the day and left. Might as well get it over with, she decided. "It's peeling and itching," she replied dryly. She had reached the front porch. Glancing over her shoulder, she saw his gaze travel to the backs of her legs as he stepped out, also.

"Looks uncomfortable," he said with gruff sympathy.

She wanted to believe he honestly cared, but she knew better. She was merely a debt he felt he needed to repay. "I'll survive," she replied coolly.

His gaze traveled upward, coming to rest on her neck and shoulders. "You should put some lotion on. You don't want to burn the rest of yourself."

In spite of her efforts to have no reaction to him, his attention caused her to feel shaky inside. Furious with herself, she regarded him frostily. "I'll stay in the shade."

He scowled impatiently. "You should take precautions. You could get skin cancer."

He was lecturing her again! Her control began to slip, and she was about to tell him that she had no need for his advice when George drove up. He issued a low wolf whistle of approval as he climbed out of the cab of his four-wheel-drive pickup. "You're looking mighty fine today, Callie," he remarked, coming toward them. His attention shifted to John as he joined them. "Seems like we're always meeting on Callie's porch." There was a question in his eyes when he glanced toward Callie.

She gave a shrug as if to say that John's presence meant nothing to her. "He just stopped by to pick up the basket I fixed for Doc and him for the picnic," she explained with an air of indifference.

"Yeah," John replied, his indifferent but polite manner once again in place. "Nice to see you again, George. Thanks, Callie," he added. Without any further conversation, he left the porch and moved toward his car.

Watching him drive away, George smiled speculatively. "I hear Jacob's daughter Ruth has been doing a lot of fetching and carrying for John while he's been working on Jacob's barn. Her divorce should be final in about a month. Looks like she's in the market for a new husband."

A hard little knot formed in the pit of Callie's stomach. It felt like jealousy. *It would be stupid to feel jealous of a man who's not the least bit interested in you,* she told herself curtly. Ignoring the irritating little pang, she forced a smile and changed the subject. "I've got our lunch packed. Shall we get going so we can corner a shady spot?"

"Sounds like a great idea to me," George replied.

As they drove into town, Callie forcefully pushed John out of her mind and concentrated on George. They discussed his crops, his horses, the weather and what kind of harvest could be expected if the dry spell they were having continued. By the time they reached the park, Callie was already running out of things to say. Breathing a mental sigh of relief, she climbed out of the truck. "There's a big old oak down by the lake," she suggested.

George looked uncomfortable. "Thought maybe we could sit under the maple up near the top of the hill."

"Sure," Callie agreed readily. She had no preference.

George's smile returned. "Great," he said, and picking up the basket and jug, began to trek across the picnic grounds.

Glancing down toward the lake, Callie suddenly understood his discomfort at her suggestion. Sally was down there under the oak with her date. But as they climbed the slight grade up to the maple, she wished she had come up with an alternative. John and Doc were already comfortably seated under the tree.

"Callie. George." Doc waved a greeting.

"Too late to change direction now," Callie muttered under her breath and waved back. Besides, why should she care if John was nearby? She'd ignore him and enjoy Doc's company along with George's.

And it should be easy, she told herself as she helped George spread their blanket. John had greeted their approach with a nod, then leaned back against the tree and returned his attention to watching a group of children playing kick ball.

Real easy, Callie assured herself, seating herself so that her back was toward John. Out of sight, out of mind.

"Heard you've got a couple of new foals that are looking real good," Doc was saying to George.

"What?" After they had finished spreading the blanket, George hadn't immediately sat down. Instead, he'd remained standing, tall and sturdy as an oak himself, staring down the hill. Jerking his attention back to Doc, he frowned self-consciously. "Oh, yeah. They're doing great." Smiling, he seated himself on the blanket.

But Callie could see that the smile was forced. Glancing down the hill, she saw Sally and her date laughing and obviously enjoying each other's company.

"Morning, John," a woman's voice sounded from behind Callie. She didn't need to turn to know who it was. She recognized the voice as belonging to Ruth Nyles, Jacob's daughter. "Didn't know what kind of lunch you and Doc might pack so I brought along a little extra."

Out of the corner of her eye, Callie saw Ruth was carrying a large picnic basket.

"Just a bit of ham and turkey, some potato salad and a cherry pie. The Doc says I make the best cherry pies in the county and you seemed to enjoy it the other day," the woman continued.

John had risen to his feet. "That's real nice of you." He smiled down at the slender brunette. "But it wasn't necessary. We've already got a lunch."

Ruth returned his smile, then said in a honey-coated tone, "It's a long day and I've noticed you have a healthy appetite."

"Looks like we had the same idea," another female voice entered the conversation.

This time Callie did glance over her shoulder. It was Sara Jennings, a tall, buxom blonde, and she had a picnic basket on her arm. "I heard Callie had a date and I didn't want you and Doc going hungry." A seductive quality entered her voice. "I'm Sara Jennings. I've been meaning to stop by Doc's place and introduce myself. It's always nice to have a new single man in town."

Sara had never been the coy type, Callie mused.

"Looks like John and I are going to be eating real well for the next few days," Doc said in an aside to Callie.

Following the line of his vision, she saw Paula Calvinau coming up the hill with a basket. Like bees to honey, she thought acidly. She glanced toward John. He was looking mildly disconcerted. Down deep, he's probably enjoying this immensely, she told herself. What man wouldn't?

As if to prove her right, his manner became more relaxed. As the three women seated themselves around him, each vying for his attention, Callie ordered herself to ignore the quartet. But instead, she found herself continuing to watch him covertly, trying to guess which woman interested him the most. It was impossible to tell. He treated each of them in the same friendly but noncommittal manner. She told herself she really didn't care if he found any of them interesting. Still, a knot formed in her stomach and when he laughed at a joke Sara told, it twisted painfully. Jerking her attention back to George, she discovered him again looking toward the oak by the lake. His jaw was set in a hard, grim line.

Callie drew a deep breath. This was going to be a very long day. Turning to Doc, she asked about the emergency call he'd had that morning.

I might as well have come with Doc, she thought later that afternoon. John was down walking by the lake with his bevy of single women and George had become more and more sullen. He'd made a weak attempt at conversation earlier but he'd barely eaten any lunch and she'd noticed that he always knew where Sally was.

When Doc was called down to the pavilion to treat a sprained ankle, knowing she wouldn't be missed, she'd gone with him. Now as she reclimbed the hill, she saw George watching Sally. Ruth's high-pitched giggle floated toward her, and out of the corner of her eye she noticed John also approaching their picnic site. She told herself that if those women wanted to make fools of themselves by so flagrantly throwing themselves at him, it didn't bother her. But by the twisting feeling in her stomach, she knew she was a liar.

As she reached the blanket, George greeted her return with a forced smile. Enough is enough, Callie decided. He didn't want to be there, and she didn't want to be there. "My sunburn is itching badly," she said apologetically. "Would you mind taking me home?"

George nearly jumped to his feet. "Sure," he agreed readily as if he'd just been sprung from a cage. "I wouldn't want you feeling uncomfortable all afternoon just for my sake."

I can't believe how ready men are to be free from my company, Callie thought bitingly as she repacked the picnic basket.

"You two are leaving?" John asked, reaching them about the time George began folding the blanket. "It's only mid-afternoon. I understand the sack races are going to start soon."

"It's a little too crowded here for Callie and me," George replied. There was the insinuation in his voice that they wanted to be alone.

Callie started to make it clear that this wasn't the case, but the sudden disapproving look in John's eyes caused her to clamp her mouth shut. He had spent the past several hours with three women hanging on to him. Besides, what she did was none of his business.

"Looks like Sally wasn't too hard to replace," Sara said with a mischievous grin.

"Looks like," George replied with the air of a man in control of his life.

Callie merely smiled and started down the hill.

"Sorry I was such rotten company today," George apologized as he drove her home.

"Maybe you should consider making up with Sally," Callie suggested, promising herself that she would never date another man on the rebound again. "All couples have their little spats."

His jaw hardened. "I don't like having ultimatums issued."

Callie raised a quizzical eyebrow. "Ultimatums?"

"Sally said we'd been going together long enough. She mentioned something about her biological clock and wanting to start a family. Then she said either I proposed and we got married or we split up," he elaborated with a growl. "I didn't mind the idea of marrying her. The truth is, I'd been thinking about it. But I didn't like being told I have to."

"You'd better start thinking about how you'll feel if she marries someone else," Callie cautioned, marveling at how thickheaded some men could be. Obviously the trouble between George and Sally was simply a matter of pride.

"Guess I'd better," he conceded grimly.

The rest of the drive to Callie's place was completed in silence. Walking her to her door, George thanked her for the picnic lunch, then left.

"So far this has been one gruesome Fourth of July," she mused dryly, watching him drive away. She shrugged as if trying to shake it off, but the image of John with the three women clinging to him filled her mind. "Might as well get some work done," she said between clenched teeth.

Attempting to push the quartet from her mind, she spent the rest of the day scraping paint. Her shoulders ached when she finally quit.

Exhausted, she showered, then pulled on an old, loose-fitting, lightweight cotton housedress. Choosing not to dry her hair with the hair dryer, she combed out the tangles, then went downstairs to the kitchen. There she fixed herself a sandwich and a glass of iced tea. Carrying them out to the front porch, she settled into the swing and ate. They were into the longest days of summer, and although it was already nearly eight, the sun would not be setting for more than another hour. Against her will she found herself wondering who John would be with when it did set. "That's none of my business," she said aloud, hoping that hearing the words would make it so. But it didn't work. Setting aside her half-eaten sandwich, she leaned back, closed her eyes and wished Doc had never brought John Smith to her home. She should have followed her instincts and refused his request. The next time Doc came asking for a favor, she'd think twice, maybe even three times, before agreeing to it.

"Have a pleasant afternoon?"

Callie's body stiffened. Had she been thinking about John so hard she was actually hearing his voice? Her eyes popped open. No, it wasn't her imagination. He was coming up the steps.

"I had a tiring one," she replied.

"Maybe you should be more careful about what kind of exercise you get," he advised frostily. He'd come to a halt at the top of the stairs and was standing, his legs slightly apart, watching her.

His manner and intonation made it clear that he thought she'd spent the afternoon in George's bed! She considered setting him straight, but she was tired and feeling cross. And hadn't he spent the day with three women catering to his every whim? "I'm always careful," she replied with a nonchalant shrug.

"Fooling around with a man on the rebound is only going to get you hurt," he continued, his voice taking on a reprimanding quality. "It should have been obvious to a blind man that he's still in love with Sally."

She scowled at him. "I'm not stupid. I know he still cares for her."

He glared down at her. "And yet you allowed yourself to be used? Damn it, Callie, I thought you had more pride than that."

"I do," she snapped, furious that he would honestly think she would have gone to bed with George. "And he didn't 'use' me as you put it. I spent the afternoon scraping paint."

Relief spread over his features, then he scowled. "Why didn't you say so in the first place?"

"Because you were having so much fun thinking the worst of me," she retorted.

Raking a hand through his hair, he regarded her with the guardedness she'd grown so used to seeing in his eyes. "I was just concerned. I don't want to see you getting hurt. I owe you a great deal."

He owed her a great deal! Her anger flared even higher. She didn't want to be a debt he was trying to repay. She wanted him gone. Well, there was one way. "A person could get the idea you were jealous," she said dryly, figuring an accusation like that would send him running.

A heavy silence suddenly descended between them and she felt like a fool. She'd been an idiot to make such a ridiculous statement. Obviously he was so dumbstruck, he didn't know how to respond. She wished she could curl up into a tiny ball and disappear in a puff of smoke.

"Jealous?" His jaw twitched as if he was fighting for control.

Her humiliation grew. He was going to laugh.

But he didn't laugh. A shadow that reminded her of the sky before a thunderstorm passed through his eyes. "Jealous?" he repeated, a bitterness coming into his voice. "I wanted to beat George to a pulp. I wanted to run after you and beg you not to leave with him. I guess that could qualify as jealous."

Callie stared at him in wide-eyed shock. For a long moment, she thought maybe she was imagining this whole thing. But the pain and anger she saw etched into his features was not her imagination.

Suddenly he turned abruptly and stalked off the porch.

In the next instant she was on her feet running after him. Reaching him, she caught the sleeve of his shirt. "I don't understand," she said shakily, coming to a halt and forcing him to stop. "As soon as your bandages were removed, you left here as if you couldn't get away fast enough, and since you've come back, you've treated me like a pest you owe a debt to."

Frustration filled his eyes as his gaze fixed on the woods beyond her. "I felt comfortable in your home,

Callie...too comfortable. At first I told myself it was just because I was so glad to be out of the hospital. But then there was you." His jaw tensed. "Whenever you touched me, there was a curiously warm sensation that spread over me. It never happened at the hospital when the nurses were taking care of me." A crooked smile suddenly played across his face. "And when you saw me in the towel, at first I thought my anger was embarrassment. Later I realized it was because I wasn't certain you would find me handsome enough." The frustration returned to his face. "By the end of the first week, I was wondering what it would feel like to hold you." His gaze shifted to her and there was a bitterness mingled with the frustration. "But I didn't know if I had the right. I could be a married man with a wife I've sworn to love and a family."

The thought of him being married brought a cold jab of fear. She knew he was the kind of man who would never turn away from his responsibilities and she would never ask him to. But to know he cared and yet they might never be able to share a life together was a bitter torture. "And so you left," she said in close to a whisper.

He nodded. "It seemed like the most honorable thing to do." A hauntedness entered his eyes. "But you were constantly on my mind. I couldn't stay away." Caressingly, he stroked her jaw. "It's been pure agony seeing you and not being able to touch you."

Agony! Callie's mind suddenly returned to the picnic. Releasing her hold on his shirt, she glared up at him accusingly. "You didn't seem to be in much pain today with those three females hanging around you."

"I barely noticed them," he growled. "All I could think of was you and George." His eyes burned into her and his hands closed around her upper arms, holding her pinned in front of him. "There is something I have to know," he demanded gruffly, his hold on her tightening possessively. "If I were free, would I have any chance with you? I know it's not fair to ask, but I've got to know."

The intensity in the dark, pleading depths of his eyes took her breath away. The memory of the three women fawning over him vanished. "Yes," she admitted, marveling at her ability to answer him coherently when her heart was pounding so loudly she was certain he could hear it. "You would have a very good chance."

There was a joy in his eyes, then they again became serious. "I would never ask you for anything less than marriage," he assured her. "I've made that promise to myself and to Doc."

Callie frowned. "Doc knows how you feel?"

John nodded. "I needed to talk to someone. I told him the day he removed my bandages. That was why he didn't insist on my staying."

That explained a lot, Callie thought, recalling Doc's remark that John's leaving might be for the best.

"It's been six weeks since the accident, and no one has made any inquiries. You'd think that if I was married, my wife would have noticed I was missing by now," John was saying in gruff tones. "But I figure I should wait six months. If no one has come looking for me by then, I'll feel free to begin a new life and assume that whatever my past is, I've made no serious commitments to anyone." Releasing her arms, he cupped her face in his hands. "I know that's a long time to ask you to wait and not get involved with anyone else, but I'm asking anyway."

His work-roughened palms against her skin caused her legs to feel weak. The fear that she could lose him from her life as quickly as he had entered it shook her. But she was willing to take that chance. "I didn't have any plans to get involved with anyone else," she replied.

Relief spread across his features. "I'm glad to hear that." His hold on her chin slackened as he began to release her. Then suddenly it tightened. "Just this once," he murmured with terse promise. "I can't resist, just one." Leaning forward he kissed her lightly on the lips.

As he lifted his head away, his breath taunted her skin. The lingering feel of his lips where they had touched hers was still warm. She ached to be in his embrace but instead she stood still, afraid to move, afraid of the strength of her longing for him.

"It's so hard to resist you when you're looking at me like that," he admonished huskily. With the groan of a man who's control was slipping, he stopped and returned for a second taste.

Callie's blood felt as if it had turned to molten lava. Unable to stop herself, this time she added her own strength to the kiss.

His thumbs massaged the sensitive cords of her neck as his effort to keep the kiss light vanished, and his mouth claimed hers hungrily.

Trailing her hands over his chest, Callie could feel his heart pounding beneath her palms. He was so sturdy, so intoxicating to touch.

"Damn!" he growled, jerking away from her. Releasing her, he took two steps back, putting a distance between them.

Startled and shaken by his abrupt desertion, Callie stood frozen. She had behaved wantonly. That was the one thing she had promised herself she would never do. She knew the consequence of letting emotions rule, and they were consequences she had promised herself she would never willingly face. Yet, she still wanted to be in his arms.

Guilt was etched into John's features. "I shouldn't have done that," he said with gruff apology.

"It wasn't entirely your fault," she heard herself admitting.

He studied her grimly. "Maybe it would be best if I went away for the next four months."

This suggestion caused a cold lump in her throat. "I suppose it might be for the best," she conceded, then added shakily, "but I don't want you to leave."

"I don't think I could go, anyway. I'd worry about you too much," he confessed. He drew a tired breath. "What are we going to do, Callie?"

For a brief moment she was tempted to tell him that she was willing to settle for whatever time they might have together, but the memories of her childhood were too strong. Besides, the look on his face told her that his conscience would torment him if he gave in and accepted such an offer. *It's better to take this slowly,* her cautious side told her, and she knew that was true. Down deep she was still finding it difficult to believe this was really happening...that he cared so deeply for her he wanted to marry her. "We could spend the next four and a half months being friends," she suggested. Her deep nagging doubts drew nearer the surface, and she heard herself adding "That will also give you time to be certain of your feelings toward me. I've heard that patients can sometimes develop an attachment to their nurses that they then mistake for something deeper."

"What I feel toward you is definitely not a nurse-patient attachment," he assured her. "And keeping my hands off you is going to be hard, but I don't want to stay away, either. Being your friend sounds like a reasonable solution."

Chapter Eight

Being "just friends" had sounded like a good idea, but it was going to be a lot more difficult than she had ever imagined, Callie thought the next night as she lay in bed staring into the dark. She'd invited John for dinner. After the meal they'd gone for a walk.

"Friends have been known to hold hands," he'd said, capturing her hand in his.

"Yes," she'd agreed. But when a friend held her hand, she'd never had warm currents racing up her arm like those she experienced from his touch. And she'd been acutely aware of the feel of his palms. Her mind had gone back to when he'd first arrived. His hands had been smooth then. Now calluses were building from the hard labor he was doing. Glancing at his arm, she had noted the rock-hard musculature. A sudden rush of excitement swept through her at the thought of being in his embrace. *Think friend,* she had ordered herself curtly.

John, on the other hand, had seemed calm and composed in spite of the contact. As they'd walked, he had talked about the barn he was building, with the interest of a man who was enjoying his work.

"Is Ruth still baking you cherry pies?" Callie had suddenly heard herself asking, then mentally kicked herself. She'd sounded jealous. Well, she was, she'd admitted.

"As a matter of fact, yes." He'd brought them to a halt and grinned down at her. "I like that note of possessiveness in your voice."

The warmth in his eyes had caused her toes to want to curl. He'd moved toward her and she'd known he was going to kiss her. Then abruptly he'd stiffened and pulled away. Guilt had shadowed his features as he'd resumed walking.

The disappointment Callie had felt was sharp and deep, but she'd hidden it.

Now, alone in her room, it came back and was followed by a sense of panic. What was she going to do if he did have a wife, and the woman came looking for him? Just the thought caused a hurt so strong it was a physical pain. Her jaw set in a grim line. "If and when it happens, I'll deal with it," she assured the darkness around her. Still, a knot of worry lingered inside. The smart thing to do would have been not to allow her feelings toward John to grow. However, she *had* fought them; she'd simply lost the battle.

Closing her eyes, Callie fell into a restless sleep.

* * *

The next evening she invited Doc to join her and John for dinner, hoping that having a third party present would prove to be a distraction.

It didn't.

Callie knew from the moment Doc arrived he had something on his mind. They were halfway through the meal when he finally spoke up. "I'm not so certain it's a good idea for the two of you to spend so much time together," he said bluntly. "I like you both and I don't want to see either one of you hurt."

John's gaze leveled on Callie. "You could be right," he admitted grudgingly. The look in his eyes told her that their walk the previous night hadn't been any easier for him than it had for her.

"I've got a cabin up in Maine," Doc continued, his attention on John. "I've been meaning to have a room built onto it. Since you seem to have a natural flair for that sort of thing, you could go up there and handle the job... supervise it and do some of the work yourself. It'd be a help to me and give you a place to stay while you give your past time to catch up with you."

After these past two days, Callie knew this would be the best solution. Still, the thought of John going away caused a sharp jab of loneliness.

"I'll think about it," John promised.

Later, after dinner, while Doc sat reading the newspaper in the living room, Callie and John went out onto the front porch. The evening shadows were only now beginning to fall. Standing, leaning against one of the square pillars that held up the roof of the porch, Callie gazed out toward the woods beyond. John stood a couple of feet away. There was no physical contact. Still, every fiber of her being was aware of his presence. Again she told herself that it would be for the best if he accepted Doc's offer and went to Maine. But she didn't want him to leave. She wanted to beg him to stay. That, however, could prove to be dangerous. Her resistance to him was low and diminishing with each passing moment. Images of her youth floated through her mind and her jaw tensed. She would not make the mistake her mother had made.

"Doc is very protective of you," he observed thoughtfully, breaking the silence between them.

"He's known me all of my life," she replied. The time had come. All day long she'd known she was going to have to tell John about herself, and the sooner the better. She'd faced rejection before. But coming from him . . . Just the thought caused her eyes to close as if she could not face that consequence. But it had to be done. Opening her eyes, she faced him. "There is something you need to know about me."

"This sounds serious," he said, studying her narrowly.

"It is." She swallowed back the lump in her throat. She would have liked to have eased into it but there was no way. "I'm illegitimate. Neither of my parents wanted me. That's why I was raised by my grandparents."

Relief showed on his face and he smiled. "Is that all?"

Callie frowned. He wasn't taking this seriously enough. "It makes a difference to a lot of people."

"Then they're very small-minded," he replied. "A baby has no choice about his parentage." His smile returned and a warmth entered his eyes. Caressingly, he traced the line of her jaw. "I thought you were going to tell me about an old love you've never completely gotten over. Then I would have something to worry about. I don't want you thinking of any other man but me."

Callie drew a shaky breath as she felt herself being drawn into the dark depth of his eyes. "I'm sure you could make a woman forget any other man," she said huskily.

"You look so delicious," he murmured, his mouth moving toward hers. But his lips had scarcely touched hers when he jerked abruptly away. "Maybe I should go to Maine. I'm not being very successful at keeping my distance."

Callie read the guilt on his face. There was also a frustration in his expression that matched her own. As light as the contact had been, the intoxicating sensation of his mouth lingered on hers and she ached for him to take her in his arms. "I suppose it would be the wisest thing," she conceded, then heard herself adding, "but I still don't want you to go." Those are probably the same words that got your mother into trouble, her inner voice warned. What really unnerved her was how much she meant them.

John's gaze softened as the frustration in his eyes grew. "Callie..." He started to reach out toward her. Suddenly he grimaced. His brow wrinkled and his eyes squeezed shut as his hand jerked back to rub the back of his neck.

Panic swept through Callie. "What's wrong?" she demanded, catching him by the upper arms to balance him as he swayed slightly.

"Just a headache," he replied through clenched teeth. "I've been having them lately, only not as bad as this one."

"Does Doc know about these?" she demanded, trying not to allow panic to take over as she eased him into a chair.

"I didn't think it was necessary to bother him about them." His words came out in clipped tones as if he was having trouble talking.

"Men!" Callie cursed, her fear increasing by the moment. "You sit here. I'm going to get Doc."

An hour and a half later Callie was pacing the floor of the waiting room in the hospital. It had taken Doc less than a minute to decide that they should take John there for tests. During the ride, Doc had tried assuring them both it was probably nothing. "You might be one of those people who have migraines," he'd said to John. "However, since you can't remember anything about your past, there's no way to know for sure. Just to be on the safe side, I'm going to have a few tests run."

But Callie knew Doc well, and she was certain he was worried.

John's "headache" hadn't gotten any better, either. By the time they had reached the hospital, she could see the lines of pain etched into his features.

She glanced at her watch. They'd taken him down to be X-rayed forty-five minutes ago. "Surely they know something by now," she muttered anxiously.

"We do," Doc said.

Callie whirled around to find him approaching. "What?" she demanded.

"It's an aneurysm," he replied, coming to a halt in front of her. "My guess is that it was caused by the accident, but it was too small and insignificant to show up in any of the tests. However, it's gotten larger and we're going to have to operate. I've called Bob and he's on his way. He's the best."

"You mean you're going to operate right now?" Callie questioned, a cold fear gripping her as the urgency of the situation became clear.

"In this case it's necessary for us to do it as quickly as possible." Doc smiled encouragingly. "He's going to be all right. I'm going to be there with him." Taking her hand, he gave it a squeeze. "And he could use a bright smile at the moment. Do you want to see him for a minute before they begin prepping him for the operation?"

Callie nodded.

John was already in a hospital gown, lying on a gurney. "Did you hear the collective groan from the nurses when I came through the door?" he asked with a crooked smile when she entered.

"It was pretty soft," she replied, attempting to match his banter.

His expression became serious. "But I assured them that you would stick around and make sure I behaved."

There was a question in his voice. Gently she stroked his jaw. "You can count on it."

"I'm glad to hear that," a female voice said from behind Callie. A teasing quality entered the voice. "But right now he's all mine."

Callie glanced toward the nurse who had just spoken. The temptation to beg her to let her stay was strong.

"Come on," Doc said, giving Callie's arm a little tug. "I've got to get scrubbed, and the nurse here has a little shaving to do." He again smiled encouragingly and winked. "John's going to get a new hairstyle."

Callie stroked John's jaw one last time and forced a reassuring smile. "See you later," she said, then let Doc guide her out of the room.

The operation lasted for hours. At one point a nurse came in and assured Callie that everything was going well. "These types of operations take a lot of time because they have to be so careful," she explained.

The little visit had helped, but not much. Callie paced the floor until her legs ached. Then she sat. Then she paced again.

Finally Doc came to find her. "It's over, and so far it looks as if everything is just fine," he informed her with an air of relief.

"Thank goodness," she breathed. But needing more reassurance, she asked anxiously, "Can I see him?"

"He's in intensive care so that they can monitor him closely," Doc explained. "And he's still groggy. But I have a feeling that seeing you might be the best medicine for him."

Callie tried not to, but she nearly forced Doc to jog down the hall. Entering the room, she approached John's bed. His eyes were closed, and she could barely see him breathing, but the monitors all around were clicking out signs of life.

"Kate's on duty," Doc said, nodding toward the windowed wall and waving at the nurse sitting on the other side with a bank of monitors in front of her. "She's top-notch."

Callie gave the young brunette a quick glance, waved as Doc had and then returned her attention to John.

"Might as well make yourself comfortable," Doc advised, pulling up a chair for her. "I'm going to get a cup of coffee, then I'll be back." He gave her shoulders a squeeze. "We'll wait this out together."

Callie barely noticed Doc leaving. Her attention was focused on John. She moved the chair nearer the bed and sat down. Doc had said the operation had gone well, but still she could not shake the fear that enveloped her. No one could be absolutely certain of the outcome of any operation, and one involving the brain was extremely dangerous. Reaching through the metal bars that had been lifted to form sides on the bed, she closed her hand around John's. The contact gave her courage, and her hold tightened.

A guttural sound came from John, and his hand folded, encasing the tips of her fingers.

Her gaze swung to his face but his eyes were still closed. "Please be all right," she pleaded quietly. Sitting there with him, it was as if they were one instead of two. If anything happened to him, it would be as if it was happening to her.

"Janice?"

Callie froze. John had spoken, but it wasn't her name he'd said. Shaken, she eased her hand out of his.

"What the hell happened?" he was demanding in a groggy, scratchy voice.

Rising, she stood looking down at him. Even though he was only half-conscious there was a commanding set to his jaw.

"You've had an operation," she replied levelly, fighting the sinking feeling in the pit of her stomach as she wondered who Janice was. Obviously she was important to him.

He groaned as his gaze narrowed and he tried to focus his eyes on Callie. "I feel as if I've been hit by a truck." His jaw tensed. "No, it was a deer. A deer ran out onto the road. I tried to miss him. Went down an incline."

His memory was back! And he had called out to a Janice. Tears burned at the back of her eyes. *You knew this could happen,* she scolded herself.

"Callie, what's wrong?" Doc demanded, entering at that moment.

"He remembers the accident," she managed, then added stiffly, "and someone named Janice."

Concern showed in Doc's eyes, then he turned his attention to his patient. Approaching the bed he gave John an encouraging smile. "I'm Dr. Marsh. Do you remember me?"

"Everything's foggy," John replied, screwing his face into an expression of concentration.

"Do you remember your name?" Doc persisted coaxingly.

"Morgan ... Morgan Evans," came the reply.

Picking up the patient chart at the foot of the bed, Doc scribbled down the name. "And do you remember where you live?"

Slowly, as if it was taking a great deal of effort to recall, Morgan gave him an address in California. "I feel groggy," he complained when he couldn't remember the zip code. His eyelids drooped, giving evidence that he was having a difficult time remaining awake.

"We'll need to contact your family," Doc persisted.

"Call Janice," Morgan instructed, and gave a number with a California area code. "She'll know what to do." He closed his eyes. "Now I've got to get some rest."

"He didn't remember either one of us," Callie said in a voice barely above a whisper. Her hands were wrapped around the top metal bar of the side of the bed, and the knuckles were white from her effort to remain in control. She should be happy for John ... Morgan, she corrected. He had regained his past and remembered his Janice, whoever she was. Callie's jaw trembled. At least this had happened before their relationship had gone any further, she told herself, trying to find a bright side.

Suddenly, Morgan's eyes opened. "Callie," he said gruffly. Then he smiled. "My Callie," he murmured, and closing his eyes, he dozed.

"I think I'd better contact this Janice and find out just exactly who she is," Doc said, frowning down at his patient, then looking worriedly up at Callie.

Callie merely nodded an acknowledgment of what he'd said as she continued to stare down at Morgan. He had remembered her and there had been a possessiveness in the way he'd said "my Callie" that warmed her. But who was Janice? She glanced up to see that Doc was already gone. Returning her attention to the sleeping man in the bed, she gently touched his cheek. Morgan Evans. The name seemed to suit him. Her mind was suddenly filled with questions. She wanted to know everything about him . . . especially who this Janice he'd first called out to was.

Striding out into the hall, she found Doc using the phone at the nurses' station. She paced behind him, listening to him explain about Morgan's amnesia and aneurysm.

"Apparently the aneurysm had something to do with the amnesia because his memory appears to have returned," he finished. After thanking the person on the other end of the line, he hung up. Turning to Callie, he smiled. "Janice is Morgan's secretary. Seems he's an architect, a very good one. A couple of months ago he finished a huge project he'd been working steadily on without a break for two years. Seems his father died of a heart attack at the age of fifty-seven from overwork. His mother insisted that this wasn't going to happen to her son. She demanded that he take a vacation. Deciding she was right, he gave Janice two months' holiday and took off on his own. At first no one worried about him. His mother apparently has a very busy social schedule and travels a great deal. Janice . . . Mrs. Sagory, is a widow. She took her two months to visit her children and grandchildren. It wasn't until she returned last week and discovered he was still gone that she began to worry. She contacted his mother, and only yesterday they hired a private firm of detectives to hunt for him.''

Callie breathed a relieved sigh. ''Then he isn't married?''

''Nope,'' Doc replied with a bright smile. His manner became businesslike. ''Janice said she'd contact Mrs. Evans. Seems Morgan's mother is right close. She's visiting friends in Washington, D.C.''

The thought of meeting Morgan's mother made Callie suddenly nervous. ''I'll go sit with him until she arrives,'' she said, starting down the hall before the sentence was finished. Back in Morgan's room, she stood by the bed, looking down at him. What would his mother think of her?

''You need to get some rest,'' Doc said insistently, entering the room.

''I want to stay with him,'' Callie argued. She wasn't certain why, but there was a small, insidious, nagging fear within her that if she left she might never see him again.

''Then at least stretch out in the lounge chair for a while,'' Doc ordered, pulling the large chair toward the bed.

Callie did feel tired. Positioning the chair so that she could see John, she sat down and, pressing against the back, caused the chair to recline.

"I'm going to go down to the doctor's lounge and get some rest," Doc told her.

Callie barely noticed him leaving. She should feel relieved to know that Morgan was a free man, she told herself, but still she couldn't shake the uneasiness that taunted her.

Callie awoke to the sound of voices speaking in hushed tones. Opening her eyes, she looked across the bed. Doc was there. With him was a woman dressed in a black evening gown that hadn't come off any rack. The emeralds and diamonds that sparkled at the woman's throat and ears weren't fakes, either. Her hair, a match in color to Morgan's, except for a scattering of gray, was flatteringly styled in soft curls swept away from her delicately featured face. The eyes were the same shape and shade as Morgan's, also. *Elegant* was the word that came to Callie's mind as she watched her.

"I can't believe this has happened," the woman was saying, disbelief mingled with the concern and fear on her face. "I suppose it sounds vain, but I've always thought of us as being a prominent family. It never occurred to me that my son could lose his identity and no one would step forth and recognize him." She shook her head. "Of course, he has always kept a low profile. As soon as he's presentable again, I'm going to take him to every social function I can find. I'll have his picture spread across every society page in the country." Promise glistened in her eyes. "He won't be able to go anywhere without being recognized."

"That brings up a question that has been bothering both me and the police," Doc said. "Why didn't he have identification on him?"

"What was he wearing?" the woman questioned with an edge of motherly impatience.

"Jeans," Doc replied.

Mrs. Evans's mouth formed a reproachful pout. "He's never liked hip wallets. He normally wears suits and carries his wallet in his breast pocket. When he dresses casually, he locks his wallet in the glove compartment of his car or tosses it onto the seat beside him while he drives." Her jaw hardened. "That's going to change, too. In fact, I'm thinking of having dog tags made up for him and insisting that he wear them at all times." She shook her head again. "I still can't believe this happened. Well, this is definitely the end of his low-profile existence."

The uneasiness Callie had been feeling earlier was growing by leaps and bounds. She shifted into a sitting position. The action caught both Doc's and the woman's attention.

"Callie," Doc greeted her with a smile. "This is Amanda Evans, Morgan's mother."

Feeling rumpled and disheveled, Callie raked a hand through her hair, trying to comb it into some sort of order as she rose. "I'm pleased to meet you," she managed levelly.

"Amanda, this is Callie Benson," Doc completed the introduction.

"You're a friend of my son's?" Amanda asked, extending a beautifully manicured hand across the bed toward Callie.

Amanda Evans's voice and manner were kind, but Callie caught the flash of guardedness in the woman's eyes. *I'm sure I'm not her idea of the ideal daughter-in-law,* Callie thought dryly. But she couldn't blame Amanda. It was only natural for a mother to want the best for her son. "I helped take care of him when he was blinded," Callie replied noncommittally.

Amanda gave Callie's hand a tight squeeze. "I want you and Dr. Marsh to know that you have my undying gratitude." Releasing Callie, she turned her attention back to the doctor. "I hope you won't be offended, but I've brought along a couple of specialists. I'd like them to take a look at Morgan, and as soon as he's able to travel I want to transfer him to Johns Hopkins in Baltimore. I'm sure you've all done a wonderful job here, but in case of complications I want him where they have all the very latest equipment."

"I appreciate your concern. Your specialists will have the complete cooperation from the staff here. As soon as Morgan is stable enough to travel, I'll arrange for the transfer," Doc replied, adding with gentle encouragement, "He's a strong man. He'll be fine."

Amanda looked lovingly at her son. "He has to be," she said with a catch in her throat.

Morgan's eyes opened slowly. "Mother?" he questioned groggily.

Amanda stroked his face. "I'm here."

"I hope you haven't tried to take over the hospital," he muttered, rewarding her with a dry smile. His gaze turned to Doc. "She looks fragile but don't let that fool you. She nearly always gets her way."

"She's behaved like a lady since her arrival," Doc assured him.

Morgan shifted so that he could look at Callie. "Mom, have you met Callie?" he asked, a tenderness entering his voice.

"Only briefly," Amanda replied, the guardedness coming back into her eyes as she too looked up at Callie.

Command entered Morgan's voice. "I want you two to get along. I plan to marry her."

Callie saw shock pass over Amanda's features. But almost immediately it was gone, replaced by a calm, quiet demeanor. "Then I shall definitely have to get to know her better," Amanda replied gently.

The thought of Amanda Evans finding out about her parentage caused a rush of panic. "I think maybe you and I should leave," Callie addressed Doc, "and let Mrs. Evans have some time alone with her son."

"It's Amanda," Amanda insisted politely, then added, "I would appreciate that."

Morgan's attention shifted to Callie. "Don't go far," he requested.

She forced a smile. "I won't. I'll just go make myself a little more presentable."

The warmth in his eyes deepened. "You look terrific to me."

Callie saw the anxious expression again pass momentarily over Amanda's features. "I'll be back," she promised, and before Morgan could say any more, she left the room.

In the hall she heard Kate talking to one of the aides. "She flew here in a helicopter with those two other doctors. I heard her saying she'd been at one of the embassies for a party. And did you see that dress and the jewels she was wearing? This Morgan Evans and his family must be loaded."

And important and influential, Callie added mentally.

Doc caught up with her in the hall. "Thought you'd be about the happiest girl in the world," he said, studying her with a worried frown.

"Things are different now," she replied. Despite her attempt to maintain a neutral facade, her chin trembled.

The worry lines on his face deepened. "Looks like we need to talk. Let me get these specialists the charts and tests they need. You go wait for me in the doctors' lounge."

Callie nodded. She needed some time alone to think. But thinking couldn't change anything, she lamented a few minutes later as she stood looking out the window of the doctors' lounge. Hearing the door open, she turned to see Doc enter. "It's not going to work out," she announced with conviction as the door closed behind him.

"What is not going to work out?" he questioned, approaching her.

He was going to make her say it. "Morgan and me," she replied.

Coming to a halt in front of her, he regarded her sternly. "There is no reason why it shouldn't."

She scowled at his obtuseness. "Of course there is and you know it!"

Concern returned to his face. "I suppose this is your way of telling me that you haven't discussed the fact with Morgan that your parents were never married." He smiled encouragingly. "I honestly don't think that's going to matter to him."

"I did discuss it with him." Callie raked a hand through her hair as she paced across the floor. Turning back to face Doc, she continued grimly, "And he assured me that it made no difference to him. But that was when he was John Smith. Morgan Evans is a whole different story. He's an important man, a prominent man with influential friends. He can't have a wife with my kind of background. Once he has time to think about it, he'll realize that." Her chin again threatened to tremble and she turned back toward the window so Doc wouldn't see. "It's best if I just end this now."

"I think you should talk to Morgan before you make any decisions," Doc advised.

Callie stared out the window with unseeing eyes, her mind going back to her youth and the whispers behind her back and the taunting she'd received from some of the children at school. "I won't place him in the position of being the target of malicious gossip."

"I'm not going to tell you that there won't be some people who will talk, but the majority will accept you as you are and they're the ones that count," Doc argued.

She wanted to believe him, but he'd never been the brunt of gossip the way she had. He didn't know how it felt. "I'll think about it," she promised.

A light rap on the door interrupted. It was followed by Amanda Evans's entrance. "I don't mean to intrude," she said apologetically, "but the nurse told me I could find the two of you in here." She turned toward Doc. "Dr. Bikala and Dr. Kasnous would like to consult with you." She smiled. "They are both very pleased with my son's care and progress." Then she turned toward Callie. "And I'd like some time for Callie and me to get to know each other better."

Callie noticed that Amanda's smile had remained on her face, but she also detected a change in it. It looked slightly forced, and there was a hint of uneasiness in the woman's eyes. It was obvious Amanda was worried that her son might be making the wrong choice. "I think that would be a good idea," Callie replied.

Doc glanced toward Callie with concern, then he said with conviction, "I'm sure the two of you will get along just fine."

"I'm sure we will," Amanda replied, her smile still in place.

For a moment Doc hesitated with his hand on the doorknob, then he left.

"Morgan has been telling me how wonderfully you looked after him when he was blinded. I know what a pain he can be when he's incapacitated. I'm sure he was difficult," Amanda said as soon as they were alone.

Callie remembered those first days, and a bitter-sweet pain filled her. "He was going through a rough time."

Amanda's smile had disappeared. The nervousness that had been behind it was now openly evident. "I hope you won't take what I'm going to say the wrong way," she began tentatively.

Inwardly Callie stiffened. She had no doubt that Amanda was going to voice an objection to her son's proposed marriage. Outwardly, however, Callie maintained a calm demeanor. "I've always felt it was best to get things out in the open."

Amanda nodded to indicate that she felt the same way. "I just don't want to see either of you hurt. But I am concerned about the true nature of your feelings for each other." Drawing a deep breath, she met Callie's gaze levelly. "Morgan has been in a vulnerable state. He's felt alone, isolated. You offered him aid and friendship." Her frown deepened. "I'm not saying that his feelings for you aren't genuine. He certainly thinks they are. I'm simply suggesting that you two don't rush into anything."

Callie couldn't deny that the woman had a valid point. She'd had the same doubts herself. "I have no intention of taking advantage of your son," she assured her tightly.

Amanda captured Callie's hand with both of hers and gave it a squeeze. "I wouldn't be talking to you like this if I thought you would. And maybe I shouldn't have said anything. It's just that all of this—discovering Morgan has been wandering around with amnesia for over six weeks and had a brain aneurysm that could have killed him—has been a shock.''

Callie looked down at the soft, beautifully manicured hands that were holding hers. The calluses on her palms seemed suddenly larger and her skin rougher. Even under the best of circumstances she would have had doubts about fitting into Morgan Evans's world. Still, there was one other thing she had to know. ''Did Morgan tell you anything about me personally or did he only talk about my taking care of him?''

''He only talked about the care you gave him,'' Amanda replied. Her hold on Callie's hands tightened and the anxiousness in her eyes increased. ''I shouldn't have said anything yet. I know my timing is all wrong.''

Callie swallowed back the lump in her throat. ''Your timing is fine,'' she managed evenly.

''I hope you don't think that I'm objecting to you,'' Amanda continued worriedly. ''I'm very shaken and am probably not expressing myself as well as I should be. Please, have lunch with me later today. I owe you a great deal, and I want to get to know you better.''

''I do understand your concern,'' Callie assured her.

Amanda gave Callie's hands a final squeeze and released them. ''I think it's time we went back in to check on Morgan.''

Hot tears were burning at the back of Callie's eyes. ''You go ahead,'' she said with a forced smile. ''I'm feeling really tired. I think I'll rest for a while.''

Amanda touched Callie's cheek gently. ''You do look exhausted. I'll tell Morgan you'll be back in after you've had a nap.''

Callie stood frozen watching the woman leave. She was afraid to say goodbye, or move, or even breathe for fear that her control would collapse and the tears would start to flow. And they did, in tiny little streams as the door closed. Turning toward the window so that anyone who entered would not see her crying, she stood weeping silently. She knew Amanda wouldn't approve of the circumstances of her birth and neither would Morgan's other family members and friends. She knew what she had to do. She'd known from the moment they had first begun to discover who Morgan Evans really was.

Chapter Nine

Callie waited until Morgan was pronounced stable enough to be moved. It wasn't easy keeping up a calm front, but Morgan slept most of the time and Amanda was so concerned about her son, she was in no mood for long conversations.

But finally the time came. "My mother has made reservations for you at the hotel where she's staying. You'll be her guest," Morgan was saying. He and Callie were alone in his room at Callie's request.

"I'm not going to go to Baltimore," she said with quiet dignity.

Morgan frowned. "Don't tell me you're afraid to fly in the helicopter? If that's the case, I'll hire a car."

"No." The word came out more sharply than she had meant it to. Think *calm*, she ordered herself. "You've gotten your life back and now it's time for me to go back to mine."

Confusion showed on his face. "I thought we were going to combine our lives."

Callie felt dizzy and realized she was holding her breath in her attempt to retain control. She took a breath and then said levelly, "Things have changed."

The confusion left his face. "I thought you cared as much for me as I cared for you. I guess I took a lot for granted."

"I did care," she choked out, unable to let him think that it had all been an act on her part. "I *do* care. I'm very glad that you are all right. I just think it's better if we both go our separate ways now."

"When you talked about a nurse-patient attachment, it wasn't me you were worried about, was it?" He regarded her dryly. "You're the kind of woman who prefers strays. As long as I had no past, I interested you. Now you find me boring."

How could he ever think of himself as boring? The urge to laugh bubbled inside of her. In a panic she realized she was on the verge of hysteria. She had never done anything that had been this painful. But it was better to make the break now. She could not face the thought of causing him embarrassment in front of his family and friends. Even more, she could not bear the rejection she might one day see in his eyes. "I just think it's better this way," she managed stiffly.

He regarded her coolly. "If that's the way you want it, then that's the way it will be."

It wasn't the way she wanted it, but it was for the best. "I'm glad you have your life back," she managed to say levelly, then with her shoulders squared she left the room.

*   *   *

Doc kept her apprised of Morgan's progress. There was only one time when she worked up enough courage to ask him if Morgan ever mentioned her or asked about her.

"No," he'd replied, watching her worriedly.

She'd shrugged to indicate it didn't matter to her. Admittedly she had been the one to break off the relationship, but it hurt to know Morgan could so quickly and so thoroughly put her out of his life. *That's what you wanted,* she chided herself. *That's what I knew he would want eventually,* she corrected.

Morgan was out of the hospital in record time. Immediately he'd flown back to California.

"I asked him to come spend a few days with me," Doc told her one Sunday evening as they sat on her porch watching the sunset. "But he said he needed to get back to work." He glanced toward her pointedly. "What I think is that the two of you need to have a talk. You're looking pale and you're not eating."

Callie's jaw tightened. Morgan hadn't tried to dissuade her from breaking off their relationship. He hadn't even asked about her once she'd walked out of his hospital room. She'd done the right thing. "We have nothing to talk about, Doc. I know that now."

He shook his head but said no more.

Later that night, however, Callie looked at herself in the mirror. She did look drawn and haggard. "That's because every room I walk into reminds of me of John...Morgan," she confessed tiredly. She'd thought that the memories would fade, but they hadn't. "What I need is a change," she decided.

The next day she went into Cumberland and got herself a job as a waitress. At least it got her out of the house, she told herself as she lay in the tub soaking her aching body the next night. Her feet were so tired she could barely wiggle her toes. Groaning, she moved her head and her gaze fell on the blue towel on the rack. It was the one Morgan had wrapped around himself that first night in her home. "Damn!" she cursed as his image again filled her mind.

The letter arrived a week later. It was from Morgan . . . a politely worded thank-you note for having ministered to him, typed by his secretary, and enclosed was a check for ten thousand dollars. The tone of the message made it clear that he saw her as an obligation that required payment and once paid could be forgotten forever. It hurt that he could so easily put her out of his life. It hurt even more that he thought she would accept money from him. Her first reaction was to rip up the check and mail it back in small pieces, but pride kept her from doing that. He might guess how much it had pained her. "And it's obvious that any feelings he had for me were not deep," she told herself. His mother had been right, his attachment to her had been born out of nothing more than the need to belong somewhere with someone. "He's probably breathing a deep sigh of relief at this very moment," she muttered as she wrote a cool but polite response refusing the money and wishing him the best.

As she sealed it, she congratulated herself for having done the right thing that day in the hospital. She had saved both of them the embarrassment and pain that would have come when he realized his mistake and wanted to be rid of her.

Two Sundays later she had even further proof that she had taken the correct path. She was standing outside the church before the services began, talking to Doc, when Jacob Kelps came up to them. "Guess that addition to that barn of mine might be famous someday, since it was built by such a prestigious architect and with his own hands, too," he said in a jocular manner. "Ruth was showing me a picture of John—" he paused and corrected himself "—Morgan this morning. There he was right on the front page of the *Washington Post*'s society section."

Callie had spent the past weeks telling herself that what Morgan did was of no interest to her. But on the way home from church she had stopped in at the drugstore and bought a paper. She told herself that she'd take a look at it later that night when she didn't have anything better to do. But the moment she got home, she carried it into the living room and sought out the society page.

There he was, dressed in a tuxedo, looking more handsome than ever. Flanking him on either side were two elegantly dressed socialites who were both smiling up at him as if entranced by his every word. The caption underneath mentioned the party they were attending and went further to name Morgan as one of the more sought-after bachelors on the social scene.

"I was right!" she stated, determined to ignore the twisting in her stomach. Taking the paper into the kitchen, she shoved it in the trash. The walls of the house suddenly seemed to be closing in on her. Going into the hall, she called the café and offered to work the afternoon shift. Her boss was ecstatic. "Sure, come on in," he'd said. "Evelyn just called in sick and we're shorthanded."

But almost as soon as she arrived, Callie wished she'd thought of some other way to spend the day. One of the nurses from the hospital was there with a few friends.

"He was a royal pain in the neck," the woman was saying emphatically, jabbing at the newspaper she was holding. "We were ready to hog-tie and gag him." Spotting Callie approaching their table, she smiled brightly and said loudly, "Then Callie took him off our hands, brave soul that she is."

Callie didn't like admitting it, but it hurt that Morgan hadn't honestly cared for her. She'd told herself a zillion times it was for the best. Still, the urge to enter into a derogatory conversation about him tempted her. But when she opened her mouth, she heard herself saying in his defense, "He was going through a difficult time."

"That doesn't mean he had to make life miserable for the rest of us," the nurse retorted with another shake of her head and returned her attention to her friends.

"He's just another spoilt rich kid," one of the men in the group observed sarcastically.

"But I'd go out with him in a minute," one of the other women interjected, taking the newspaper and giving Morgan a closer look.

Spoilt rich kid. That wasn't Morgan. He'd proven himself to be a decent, honest, hardworking man. The temptation to tell her customers that they were mistaken, that they didn't know him and shouldn't be talking about him, was strong. But she held her tongue. They'd already moved on to another subject and would probably never think of Morgan again. She wished she could do the same thing. What she did do was to trade tables with one of the other waitresses.

Driving home that night, she again told herself how lucky she was to have broken off with him when she had, saving them both the pain that the realization he wasn't really in love with her would have caused. "We're both where we belong, each in our separate worlds," she said with conviction. She just wished her world didn't feel so empty.

It hadn't felt empty before Morgan had come into her life. She had, in fact, been content. Now there was a restlessness in her as if she was incomplete. *It will pass,* she assured herself.

But no matter how busy she kept herself, every once in a while his image would come into her mind.

Then the second letter from him came. It was a crisp fall day near the middle of October. The leaves were changing and the air was fresh. She'd spotted the letter immediately when she'd pulled her mail out of the mailbox that afternoon. Walking back up the drive toward the house, she'd considered sending it back unopened. She'd set him free and he was happy. Why couldn't he leave her alone?

When she reached the house, she tossed the rest of the mail in on the hall table, then, still holding his letter, she went out onto the porch and sat down. Propping her legs up on the rail, she scowled at the envelope. It probably contained another check, she decided, recalling how stubborn he could be when he set his mind to something. Well, she could be just as stubborn. If it was a check, he was going to get it back and this time with a note asking him to leave her alone.

But there was no check inside. What was there was a shock. Panic filled her as she read the letter. Her feet came off the railing with a loud plop and she sat straight up and reread it. "He can't be serious!" she exclaimed after the second reading.

She read it a third time. He wanted to come back and live here under her roof. It was bothering him that he was supposed to have conversed with a ghost and he wanted the opportunity to see Chester.

I've always been a very practical man and this business about the ghost has been nagging at me. I'm designing a home for a couple near Washington, D.C., and feel this would be a good opportunity to give Chester another chance to show himself to me. To that end, I would like to rent my old room. Since he would not show himself while I was staying with Doc, and since Doc has never seen him, I can only assume he prefers to converse only with residents in your home.

My secretary, Janice Sagory, will be accompanying me. Neither of us wants to be a bother so I have arranged for Doc's housekeeper to come over once a week and clean. I can also make arrangements for her to cook dinner if you would like. Otherwise I will pay you extra for providing meals.

Unless I hear from you, we will be arriving on the twentieth of October.

There was no salutation at the end, just his signature... Morgan Evans.

"He can't!" she snapped. It was taking all of her effort to put him out of her life. He couldn't simply invite himself back in again. She forced herself to think. The twentieth was in four days. She glanced at her watch. It was still mid-morning in California and a weekday. His secretary should be in the office. Taking a calming breath, she rose from her chair. "I'll go in and call her and tell her that it's impossible for them to come," she said in rational tones.

Carrying the letter inside, she dialed the number on the letterhead. Her breath threatened to lock in her lungs as it rang.

"Morgan Evans's office," a woman's voice intoned from the other end of the line. "Janice Sagory speaking."

"This is Callie Benson," Callie replied levelly. "I..."

"Miss Benson," Janice cut in politely but firmly, "please hold."

Before Callie could protest, the line went silent. Under normal conditions Callie didn't like being put on hold. Under these conditions, every fiber in her body rebelled. She was tempted to hang up but that wouldn't serve her purpose. She had to make it clear that these people couldn't come to her home.

"Callie."

Callie froze. It was Morgan's voice. She didn't want to talk to him, not personally. Her hand jerked the receiver away from her ear and started to return it to the cradle. But before she could slam it down, she stopped herself. That was the coward's way out. Besides, what choice did she have? If she didn't tell him he couldn't come, he'd be on her doorstep in four days. Slowly she raised the receiver back to her ear. "Morgan?"

"Yes, it's me. Can I assume this call is in reference to the letter I sent you?" he replied coolly.

"It is very inconvenient for you to come here." She said the line she had been rehearsing mentally.

His voice became brusquely businesslike. "I'm sure you can understand how conversing with a ghost can, pardon the pun, haunt a person. I need some time to sort this out, and since Chester resides in your home, that seems to be the only place to do it." There was resignation in his voice that suggested he would have preferred to meet Chester at the doors of hell than in her home, but he had no choice. "Janice and I can take care of ourselves, and as I mentioned, I've hired Doc's housekeeper to take care of any extra cleaning that's needed because of our stay. You can go on about your life as if we're not even there."

Go on with her life as if they were not even there? Morgan might be able to put her out of his mind easily but just the sound of his voice brought back a flood of old memories and she felt all shaky inside. "I can understand how you feel. However—" Callie began.

"Fine," Morgan cut her short. "We'll be seeing you in four days."

Callie stared at the phone as the line went dead. People in California certainly had an abrupt way of ending conversations, she mused dryly, fighting down a fresh rush of panic. He was determined to come. But only because of Chester. Down deep she experienced a sharp pang of hurt, and scoffed at her image in the hall mirror. "You idiot!" She hated admitting it, but for one brief second when she'd first heard his voice, she'd let herself hope that he might have been missing her and was using Chester as an excuse to see her again. His tone and manner, however, had immediately dissuaded her of that notion. It was clear she didn't interest him at all.

She dropped the receiver into the cradle, then went upstairs. Going into the room he had used, she crossed to the closet and opened the door. Her grandfather's bathrobe was hanging there. Her chin threatened to tremble as she reached out and touched it. Maybe Morgan's coming here was a good idea. Seeing him again might be the way to get him out of her system. After all, she had fallen in love with John Smith. Morgan Evans would not be the same man. All she needed was to see that John Smith was gone forever and she could put him to rest once and for all.

"And one thing's for sure," she said, grabbing the robe off the hanger. "Morgan Evans isn't going to need this old thing."

But as she stood clutching the faded garment, hot tears suddenly welled in her eyes. For the first time she allowed herself to admit how much she missed John Smith. It was as if a part of her had been ripped away.

"No sense in crying over something that was never meant to be," she scolded herself, and forced herself to remember the newspaper clipping of Morgan Evans with the socialites. Her shoulders straightened and she blinked back the tears. "It's obvious I made the right decision."

It was four days later. The silver Mercedes glistened in the late-afternoon sun. She watched from the front door as Morgan Evans lifted the suitcases out of the trunk and carried them toward the house. In his tailored suit he looked totally out of place in this rural environment. This was not the man she had fallen in love with, she told herself. Still, seeing him was more difficult than she had ever imagined it could be.

She glanced around at the interior of the hall. Everything was polished. In truth, the whole house was spotless. In a fit of anxiety, she'd cleaned it from top to bottom. The aroma from the dinner she was cooking filled the air. It was a pot roast, and that morning she'd baked an apple pie. They had been John's favorites, but she doubted that Morgan Evans would enjoy such a simple menu.

"Something smells very good," Janice Sagory said as Callie opened the door and stepped aside to allow them to enter.

The woman was trying to hide it, but Callie could see that she was uneasy.

"I told you that you didn't need to go to any trouble for us," Morgan said with stiff politeness as he followed his secretary inside. "We could have gone into Cumberland for dinner."

There was a cold air of authority about him and a hint in his manner as if he found the fact that she had cooked dinner for them annoying. There was no sign of the John Smith she knew in Morgan Evans. Even his features seemed different...harsher. The knowledge that she had been right buoyed Callie. She met his coolness with indifference. "I thought you'd want to see Doc so I invited him to dinner. But if you'd rather eat in Cumberland, go ahead."

Morgan shrugged. "You're right, I would like to see Doc," he replied in a tone that suggested seeing Doc was the only reason he would consider staying for dinner. He glanced toward the rarely used parlor. "Would you mind if I set up my drafting table and Janice's computer in there?"

"In there is as good a place as any." This exposure to him was going to be good for her, she told herself. A few days of Morgan Evans and she'd be able to put John Smith to rest for good.

He gave a businesslike nod, then continued through the hall and up the stairs.

Janice frowned worriedly at his departing back. "Don't know what's gotten into him lately. He used to have better manners." Glancing toward Callie she said apologetically, "We've had a long day."

Callie wanted to tell the woman not to make any excuses for Morgan's behavior. She preferred him that way. But instead she said evenly, "Let me show you to your room."

"I have to admit that I'm a little nervous." Janice glanced uneasily around her as they ascended the stairs. "I don't usually let ghost stories spook me, but when Morgan told me that we were coming here because he'd actually conversed with one, that shook me. Normally it's our more unusual clients, the ones that are a bit eccentric, who make claims like that. I never thought I'd hear those words coming out of Morgan's mouth." Janice suddenly flushed. "Not that you seem eccentric or anything." They had reached the door of Janice's room. Coming to a halt, she grimaced self-consciously. "I'm sorry. I'm rattling on. Please don't pay any attention to anything I've said. It's been a very tense day."

The door across the hall opened and Morgan stepped out. He scowled impatiently at his secretary. "I've told you that you have nothing to fear from Chester."

"I doubt that you'll even see him," Callie added, momentarily shaken by Morgan's presence. He'd taken off his suit coat and tie and unfastened the top two buttons on his shirt. His hair was slightly rumpled as if he'd run his fingers through it and he suddenly reminded her of John. Then she forced herself to meet his eyes and the coldness she saw there chilled her. John Smith was dead. Morgan Evans was a stranger and one she was having no trouble disliking. It occurred to her that Chester would not like him, either. She continued to regard Morgan with the same coldness with which he was regarding her. "There is also the possibility he won't choose to show himself to you again."

He shrugged. "This job should take a month. Once it's over, if I haven't seen him again, I'll conclude that he was a figment of my imagination brought on by the blow to my head.''

Callie wished he had already accepted that explanation. It would have saved them both from this encounter. But he hadn't. Determined to look on the bright side, she again told herself that having Morgan Evans around should definitely cure her remaining longings for John Smith. ''I have to go see to my dinner,'' she said brusquely. She left them and went back downstairs.

As she checked on the roast, she mentally promised dire consequences to Doc if he didn't show up for this meal, then she scowled at her own cowardliness. ''I don't need any protection from Morgan Evans,'' she assured herself. But the sound of familiar footsteps coming through the dining room caused her back muscles to tighten. She knew it was Morgan, and it irritated her that she knew. She didn't want to be that aware of him.

''I noticed you've set the dining-room table,'' he said, entering the kitchen as she closed the oven and straightened. ''I don't think I've ever eaten in there.''

He had changed into jeans and a sweatshirt and for a moment, it was as if John was there. But he wasn't John, he was Morgan Evans. She forced herself to once again picture him in his tuxedo, sandwiched between the two socialites. ''It seemed the most appropriate for a man who makes the front page of the society section of the *Washington Post*,'' she replied. Immediately she wished she'd said anything but that.

His gaze steadied on her and he raised a questioning eyebrow. ''I didn't think you ever read the society page of the *Washington Post*. In fact, I don't remember you ever purchasing that particular newspaper.''

Pride refused to allow her to let him think that she was interested in what he had been doing since they had parted. ''Jacob brought your picture to everyone's attention,'' she said with forced nonchalance. ''He said he was thinking of having a plaque put up on his barn.''

True amusement glistened in Morgan's eyes and he laughed. ''Maybe I'll even pay for it. That's the first time I've wielded a hammer since I got out of college. Despite all the times I smashed my fingers, it felt good.''

Callie's heart lurched. That was John's smile and his laugh.

''I'll have to go by and see Jacob while I'm here,'' he finished thoughtfully, then suddenly the smile was gone as quickly as it had appeared, and Morgan Evans was back, regarding her with cool indifference. ''In the meantime, I was wondering if I could get a glass of water. I have a headache.''

Callie froze with fear. ''Are you certain it's just a headache?''

He frowned impatiently. ''I appreciate your show of concern,'' he said in a voice that suggested he thought it was merely superficial. ''But, yes, I'm certain it's only a headache.''

It hurt that he thought she honestly didn't care. ''My concern was genuine,'' she said stiffly, going to the cupboard and taking out a glass.

''I apologize if I made you think I thought otherwise.''

The cynical edge in his voice irritated Callie. She'd freed him to go back to his former life unencumbered by a wife who would have caused him embarrassment, and he had gone and not looked back. He had no right to think of her as callous. She spun around to face him, only to discover that he was watching her with an air of indifference. He didn't care whether she was truly concerned or not. Biting back the protest on the tip of her tongue, she handed him the glass.

As he took it, his fingers brushed against hers. To her dismay a rush of heat spread up her arm.

"Thanks," he muttered, almost jerking away as if he found the contact unpleasant. Going over to the sink, he ran himself a glass of water.

I am not attracted to Morgan Evans, she told herself sternly. He most certainly was not attracted to her. The moment he'd taken his aspirin, he left the kitchen as if he couldn't get away fast enough.

"Chester!" she seethed under her breath. "Would you *please* show yourself so he'll leave? You could do me this one little favor this time. His being back here is all your fault. You owe me this much. All these years you've refused to show yourself to Doc and yet you came around and actually talked to Morgan Evans."

Out of the corner of her eye she caught a shadow but when she turned it was gone. "Your little games are getting on my nerves," she warned and could have sworn she heard a faint boyish giggle. Clearly, Chester was not going to cooperate and help her get Morgan Evans out of her life.

To her relief Doc showed up even earlier than she'd expected. But the relief was short-lived. The pleasure on Morgan's face at seeing Doc was genuine, and as the two men greeted each other and began to talk, Callie again saw John Smith in Morgan Evans.

Escaping into the kitchen, she tried not to recall other dinners with her and Morgan and Doc, and especially those with only her and Morgan.

She was mixing the corn bread when Janice came into the kitchen. The secretary had changed into a white and lavender slack-and-sweater outfit. "Morgan said we should dress casually," she said as she entered.

"You look very nice," Callie replied to the question in the woman's voice.

"I was wondering if I could help," Janice offered.

"I really have everything in hand," Callie replied. "Have you met Doc? He and Morgan are in the living room."

"No, I haven't met him yet. I heard the men when I came down. They seemed to be so involved in conversation, I didn't want to interrupt." A shadow of anxiousness came into the secretary's eyes as she moved closer to the table where Callie was working. "I was wondering about this ghost of yours. Is he...does he..." She paused as if uncertain how to phrase her question.

Callie paused in her measuring and smiled at the woman encouragingly. "He's perfectly harmless." Just in case Chester was listening, she added pointedly, "But he can be a nuisance."

Janice breathed a sigh. "I didn't know if he was the kind who threw tantrums and began rattling dishes and tossing furniture."

"Mostly he just flits in and out. Morgan is the only person I know of, besides my grandmother and me, that he has even shown himself to. In fact until Morgan showed up, Chester was extremely quiet. He normally didn't even talk to me. He still doesn't," Callie elaborated.

Janice shook her head. "I find it hard to believe... Morgan Evans conversing with a ghost. He's such a practical, level-headed man. I suppose that would explain why he's been so out of sorts since his return." Janice studied Callie closer. "The truth is, when he insisted on coming here, I thought maybe there was some unfinished business between you and him."

"There is no unfinished business between Callie and myself," Morgan's voice sounded from the doorway.

Callie jerked around to see him entering the room with Doc following. There was a grim finality in his voice. *You knew it was over,* Callie admonished herself, trying to ignore the sharp twist in her stomach. *But it hurt, hearing him say it like that, as if he found the thought of having anything to do with her distasteful.* Her shoulders straightened with pride.

"No, nothing," she confirmed. For one brief moment she forced herself to meet his cool gaze, then quickly returned her attention to her cooking.

"I'm Howard Marsh," Doc said, breaking the sudden heavy silence that descended over the kitchen.

Moving toward Janice, he extended his hand. "Everyone calls me Doc."

"And I'm Janice Sagory," the secretary said, her gaze traveling from Callie to Morgan and then to Doc. As she accepted the handshake, her gaze shifted back to Morgan and she raised a skeptical eyebrow. "Nothing?"

For a moment his eyes shifted to Callie, then back to his secretary. "Nothing," he replied firmly.

Callie caught the exchange out of the corner of her eye and her mouth formed a hard, straight line. Again he was proving that she had made the right decision. If he'd ever honestly cared for her, he couldn't have stopped caring so easily.

"I've been telling Morgan that he'll have to come over and do some fishing. I hope you'll come with him," Doc addressed Janice, obviously changing the subject.

"I'm not much of a fisherwoman," she replied.

"Then you and I can sit on my deck and watch while Morgan fishes."

Callie glanced toward Doc. He was flirting with Janice. Well, why not? Janice was a good-looking woman. Callie just hoped he had a lot better luck with his love life than she had with hers.

"Now that you've met Janice, I suggest we go back into the living room and let Callie finish dinner," Morgan said, already moving toward the door.

Doc offered Janice his arm.

"Are you certain I can't help?" Janice asked once again.

"I'm certain," Callie replied.

Smiling up at Doc in a manner that suggested she found him interesting enough to want to get to know him better, Janice accepted his arm and allowed him to escort her out while Morgan held the door open.

Callie glanced toward their departing backs to find Morgan looking back at her, his expression shuttered. Turning away, he followed the others, letting the door swing shut. *He's probably wondering what in the world he could have seen in me,* she mused, returning her attention to the corn bread.

The rest of the evening passed smoothly enough. It was clear that Doc found Janice interesting, and she seemed to enjoy his company. Callie said very little, letting the others carry the conversation.

When Morgan began to talk about the house he was designing for his newest client, she could see how much he loved his work. She also found herself recalling his first day in her home. The way he had memorized the layout of the place and understood the use of each room should have given her some clue that he'd had something to do with building homes or designing them.

Doc left around ten and Callie immediately excused herself. "I've got the breakfast and lunch shift tomorrow. I need to be at work by six," she said, and, wishing Morgan and Janice a good-night, she went up to bed.

But sleep didn't come easily. She tossed and turned and couldn't get comfortable. She heard Janice come upstairs almost immediately, and like someone waiting for the second shoe to fall, she listened for Morgan's footsteps. But he didn't come up. Finally she fell into a restless sleep.

It was a little after 2:00 a.m. according to the clock on her bedside table when she awoke with a monster of a headache. She'd been dreaming, but she couldn't remember the dreams, only an array of faces including Doc's and Morgan's and the two socialites from the newspaper clipping. There was also the lingering sensation of frustration and sadness. For a few minutes she lay there trying to go back to sleep but her head ached too badly.

Finally she dragged herself out of bed. Remembering she was not alone in the house, she grabbed her robe from the closet, then went into the bathroom. The bottle of aspirin in the medicine cabinet contained one pill. That wasn't enough. Cursing under her breath, she headed for the kitchen. There was a new, full bottle down there.

She moved quietly so as not to disturb the others in the house. But as she reached the foot of the stairs and started across the hall, the floorboard near the entrance to the living room creaked. Startled, she gasped and spun around to discover Morgan standing in the doorway. All of the lights in the house had been out. She'd been forced to flip on the one that illuminated the stairs and the entrance portion of the hall to light her way. Because of that she'd assumed that he'd already gone to bed. But he hadn't. He was still wearing the jeans and shirt he'd worn at dinner, and the shadows under his eyes gave evidence that he hadn't slept yet.

"I woke up with a headache," she said, feeling the need to say something. "The bottle of aspirin in the bathroom was nearly empty." He stood watching her, saying nothing, and her already tense nerves tensed further. "I didn't see any lights on down here. I thought you'd gone to bed."

He gave a shrug. "I learned to get around in this house without any sight," he reminded her.

Vividly, memories again flooded over her.

"I always wondered what you looked like when you were running around the house in the night or early morning," he continued, a gruffness coming into his voice.

Even wearing the heavy flannel gown and her robe, she could feel his gaze like a physical touch as it traveled over her.

Suddenly he abruptly stalked toward the stairs. "Guess Chester isn't going to show up tonight," he muttered impatiently. Without giving her a second glance, he added, "'Night, Callie," as he passed her.

Obviously he didn't like what he saw, she mused. Glancing in the hall mirror, she couldn't blame him. The circles under her eyes were darker than those under his. Her hair was a tangled mess and her clothing was, at best, nondescript. The pain in her head pounded even harder. Continuing into the kitchen she took the aspirin. Good thing I have a job, she thought on her way back upstairs. At least she could be gone by the time he got up in the morning, and she wouldn't have to face him during the day.

"Dammit, Chester. Show yourself and get this over with," she ordered in curt low tones as she climbed back into bed.

Chapter Ten

The next morning Callie was on her way to work before either Morgan or Janice was up. She left a pot of coffee staying hot in the percolator, and she'd stocked her refrigerator with the foods John had liked for breakfasts and lunches. If Morgan Evans had different tastes, he'd have to go shopping for himself. And he probably would, she added as she pulled out onto the main road. He hadn't eaten much at dinner the night before. John had always taken seconds, and sometimes thirds, of her pot roast. Morgan also hadn't shown much interest in her apple pie. "He obviously has much more cultivated taste buds now than he had as John Smith," she observed dryly. She cocked a cynical eyebrow. Cultivated or not, tomorrow he was going to get that leftover pot roast in the form of beef pot pie.

"Even if Chester doesn't show up, my plain country cooking might drive him out," she muttered as she pulled into the parking lot of the café.

But he was still there when she got home from work late that afternoon. As she passed by the parlor, she couldn't stop herself from pausing to glance inside. Dressed in jeans and a heavy pullover sweater, he was seated at his drawing table, his jaw set in concentration. The table had its own lamp but was also placed near a window for better lighting. As she watched, he straightened and stretched his back. The sudden urge to rub his shoulders swept through her. *How can you continue to have such foolish reactions?* she scoffed at herself. However, that might just send him running, she mused sarcastically, again wishing he would leave.

"I hope you don't mind." Janice's voice broke into Callie's thoughts.

She turned her attention toward the other end of the room to discover the secretary seated in one of the kitchen chairs at the oak table that was normally situated against the wall on that side of the room. The table had been pulled out so that Janice could sit behind it and face the interior of the room. The secretary's computer and printer had replaced the framed photographs, hurricane lamp and crocheted doilies that usually occupied the polished surface.

"I confiscated your chair and table," Janice continued apologetically.

"That's fine," Callie replied, noticing that the photographs had been carefully added to those already on the mantel over the fireplace, and the doilies and hurricane lamp now resided on a table near the far window. Feeling a prickling on her neck, she glanced over her shoulder. Morgan was watching her and there was anger in his eyes. Obviously he didn't like his work disturbed. "I didn't mean to interrupt," she said stiffly.

A polite mask descended over his features. "It's your home," he replied with a shrug, returning his attention to his drawing.

Callie swung her attention back toward Janice to find the secretary regarding her with a contemplative expression. "I'm planning on having roast chicken for dinner," she said, breaking the silence that had fallen over the room.

"Sounds delicious," Janice replied with a polite smile.

Morgan said nothing.

Obviously he and John Smith have radical differences in their taste buds, Callie quipped to herself as she exited the room without so much as a glance in his direction. Her roast chicken was another thing John had always enjoyed.

Well, I'm not trying to please Morgan Evans, she reminded herself as she changed into jeans and a sweatshirt. It had only been politeness that had caused her to plan John's favorite meals, anyway. And she was being practical. Meals no one liked produced a lot of leftovers. "At this rate, my freezer should be well stocked with precooked food by the time they leave," she muttered.

Callie had put the chicken in the oven and was peeling potatoes when a knock sounded on the front door. By the time she reached the hall, Janice was opening the door to greet their caller.

It was Ruth Nyles. "You must be Janice Savory, Morgan's secretary," the woman said with a bright smile. Seeing the surprise on Janice's face, she added, "News travels fast around here." Leaning to one side, she peeked around Janice. "When I heard Morgan was back in town, I decided that the neighborly thing to do would be to bake him a pie. He always loved my cherry pies."

Callie had stopped when she saw Janice answering the door. Now she stood watching from a distance. If Ruth thought that Morgan Evans would be interested in her pie, she was in for a shock.

"Please, come in," Janice offered, stepping aside to allow the woman to enter.

Callie had again started toward them when Morgan came out of the parlor. "Did I hear you say you had brought one of your famous cherry pies?" he questioned Ruth with a welcoming grin.

Still a few feet from the trio by the door, Callie again stopped. Her stomach twisted into a knot. He actually sounded as if he was pleased.

"Thought I should do something to welcome you back," Ruth replied, her smile broadening even further. Then her lips formed a petulant pout. "You left so suddenly, I didn't even get a chance to say goodbye."

"I did leave a little more abruptly than I had planned," he conceded, adding, "but I had a life I needed to resume."

"Well, I'm glad you've come back for a while."
Ruth smiled seductively as she handed him the pie.
"And I hope you'll have time to come by for dinner.
How about this Sunday?"

"I've already promised Doc I'd go fishing with
him," Morgan said politely. "But I appreciate the invitation."

"Some other time, then?" Ruth coaxed.

Callie saw him hesitate. She was certain he wasn't
really interested in Ruth. None of the women around
here were sophisticated enough for his world. Cynically she watched and waited. John Smith would never
lead a woman on intentionally. However, she didn't
know about Morgan Evans. It occurred to her that he
could be a wanton womanizer. That would definitely
cure her for good.

"I'm on a very rushed schedule," he said after a
moment.

Ruth did not hide her disappointment well. "Too
bad," she said with an exaggerated sigh. "I was planning to make all of your favorites." Then with another sigh, she said a quick goodbye to Janice and
swished out of the house, swinging her hips in an exaggerated manner as if to show Morgan what he was
missing.

Callie was a muddle of emotions. A part of her was
ecstatic that he had chosen not to spend time with
Ruth. Another part almost wished he had and proven
himself to be a cad. *What he does shouldn't make any
difference to me either way!* she told herself curtly. He
had no interest in her, and it was stupid of her to have
any interest in him. She'd been in love with John

Smith, and John Smith was gone. Turning sharply, she went back into the kitchen.

The door had barely swung closed behind her when it opened again and Morgan entered, carrying the pie.

Callie told herself to be quiet. But she had worked hard on the apple pie she'd made yesterday, and he'd barely touched it. The insinuation in his voice in the hall had been that he could hardly wait to devour Ruth's pie. Almost as if it was someone else speaking, she heard herself saying sarcastically, "Would you like a piece of that pie now, or can you bear to wait until after dinner?"

He regarded her dryly. "Why, Callie Benson, I could almost get the impression you were jealous."

Callie's body stiffened. She'd thrown that accusation at him once, and the results had been a shock...a very pleasant shock. But this was different. He was mocking her. He'd made it clear since his arrival that he found her an irritant. "I'm not," was all she could think to say. Picking up the potato peeler, she again began to prepare dinner.

For a long moment she could feel him watching her. Then she heard him move to the counter, put down the pie and leave.

"You idiot!" she scolded herself under her breath. She had been jealous. But to let him guess that would have been embarrassing to both of them. He is not John Smith, she reminded herself. Drawing a shaky sigh, she promised herself that she would be more careful in the future.

By the time she put dinner on the table, Callie was certain she had her emotions under control. If he wanted to eat the entire cherry pie for dessert that would be fine with her.

"Everything smells delicious," Janice said as she seated herself.

"Callie has always proven to be an excellent cook," Morgan commented as he joined the women.

Shocked by what sounded like an actual compliment, Callie glanced toward him, but the expression on his face was one of cool detachment. Obviously he was simply attempting to be polite.

She'd again chosen to eat in the dining room. The more formal surroundings helped her to keep the differences between John Smith and Morgan Evans in a sharper perspective.

"Been seeing much of George?"

Callie had been serving herself some mashed potatoes. Freezing in mid-motion, she looked toward Morgan. He'd asked the question in a perfunctory sort of way as if merely making conversation. But the subject matter surprised her. Until now he'd avoided asking anything personal. Could it be that he did still harbor some feelings for her? "No. He married Sally a couple of weeks ago," she replied, finishing serving herself and passing the bowl to Janice.

Picking up the plate of chicken, Morgan scanned it thoughtfully. "Too bad. But I'm sure some other stray will come along soon."

"I don't—" Callie started to defend herself. But Morgan's attention was on the chicken, and there was an apathy in his manner that made it clear he had no real interest in whatever she was going to say. *I suppose his pride demanded that he get one little jab in,* she mused. She couldn't honestly blame him for that. Even if it had proven to be the right thing to do and he was glad to be rid of her, she *had* walked out on him. Janice, on the other hand, was watching her sharply. Callie took a calming breath, then said evenly, "If someone comes along I want to share my life with, that will be fine. If not, I'm quite content."

Content. The word echoed in her mind. That was the biggest lie she had ever told. There was an emptiness in her she was afraid would never go away. Her jaw tensed. *It will pass,* she assured herself and tried not to remember how it had felt to be in John Smith's arms. He was gone forever. She forced herself to look toward Morgan. There she found confirmation in the coolness of his eyes and the hard set of his jaw.

Out of the corner of her eye Callie noticed Janice regarding her and Morgan with a speculative frown. For a moment the secretary looked as if she was going to say something, then she returned her attention to her food. Callie breathed a sigh of relief. She was in no mood to fend off any inquiries or comments Janice might have had regarding what had just passed between her and Morgan.

Determined to be as indifferent to Morgan's presence as he was to hers, Callie asked Janice if she had any favorite recipes. This initiated a conversation between her and the secretary about cooking, which she managed to keep going during the entire main course.

Then it came time to serve the dessert. Callie carried out Ruth's cherry pie and what was left of her own apple pie. But when she stood poised to serve, the words to ask Morgan which he preferred stuck in her throat. It's not as if you're asking him to choose between you and Ruth, she admonished herself, but her nerves remained taut. Suddenly she was cutting a huge slice out of the cherry pie. "I'm sure you want this," she heard herself saying with forced cheerfulness, as she dished the gigantic wedge onto one of the plates, then handed it to Morgan. He hadn't shown much interest in her apple pie, and she was forced to admit that down deep she didn't want to hear him asking for the cherry pie.

He accepted it without comment and began to eat.

The temptation to pour the rest of it in his lap was strong. That would be idiotic, she scolded herself. Turning toward Janice, she smiled and asked the secretary which she preferred.

Janice looked uncomfortable as her gaze traveled from Morgan to Callie once again. "I think I'll skip dessert tonight," she said. "If you two will excuse me, I've got a phone call I need to make."

Callie would have liked to have fled the room, too, but pride wouldn't allow her. "I think I'll try the cherry pie myself," she said with schooled casualness. But as she began to eat, the image of him smiling down at Ruth taunted her and the food threatened to stick in her throat. "This is too sweet for me," she announced abruptly and escaped into the kitchen.

But the escape wasn't complete. She had just begun to wash the pots and pans when Morgan entered carrying a load of dishes.

That was something John would do. A hard lump formed in Callie's throat. But John was gone. He'd never been real! "There's no reason for you to do that," she said with stiff dismissal as he put them on the table.

"I never meant for you to wait on Janice and me," he replied over his shoulder, already heading back toward the dining room.

Watching him carry in a second load of dishes, Callie wished he would stick to her image of Morgan Evans. She had been able to convince herself that John Smith was as much a ghost as Chester, but her heart still hadn't let him go.

"I'll dry."

Every muscle in Callie's back knotted. "There is no need for you to do that."

"I've done it before," he replied, ignoring the curt note in her voice and picking up a dish towel.

Callie's control went. "No." She turned toward him and faced him squarely. "John Smith dried dishes. *You* never did."

Anger sparked in his eyes, then it was gone, replaced by a cold callousness. "You're right," he growled. "I'm not John Smith. I'm no stray. I'm no phantom surrounded by mystery. I'm just a plain, ordinary man." Throwing the dish towel on the counter, he headed for the door.

Plain. Ordinary. Those were not words she would ever use to describe him, Callie thought, watching him numbly.

But before he could complete his exit, Janice entered. Her gaze traveled from Morgan to Callie and she frowned. "For two people who don't have any unfinished business, there seems to be a great deal of tension in this house." She held up a cautioning hand toward Morgan when he began to speak. "And don't try to tell me that it has anything to do with your ghost." Again her gaze traveled between them. "To be honest, it's getting on my nerves. Doc is on his way over. He's going to drive me up to Gettysburg to spend the weekend with my son and his family. I hope you two will use this opportunity to clear up whatever is between you, because I do not enjoy feeling like a buffer between two war zones."

Morgan's gaze narrowed on Callie. "Callie prefers phantoms to real people. She and I have no unfinished business." Before either woman could respond, he stalked out of the kitchen.

Janice frowned at the door as it swung shut behind him, then she turned toward Callie. "I don't understand what is going on here, but I hope the two of you can work it out. In the meantime, you don't need me around. I'm going to pack."

Callie stood mutely as the woman left. The contempt in Morgan's eyes had been blatant. He despised her. His attitude wasn't fair and neither was his accusation, she fumed defensively. What she'd done, she'd done for him, and he certainly hadn't suffered. She could still see him at his posh society function with the two socialites smiling seductively up at him.

Mechanically she began to wash dishes. Tears burned hot in her eyes. She wanted to seek him out and tell him that he was wrong... that she wanted a flesh-and-blood man's arms around her. Her jaw trembled. She wanted his arms around her. She'd worked hard to convince herself that Morgan Evans and John Smith were two different people. But down deep inside she knew they were basically the same man. She'd seen it when Morgan was with Doc and in the way he treated Janice . . . not as hired help but as a friend. There was just one little difference between Morgan and John—the only emotion Morgan Evans felt for her was disdain. "I did the right thing," she stated through clenched teeth. She just wished it would stop hurting so much.

She heard Doc's car drive up and said a silent prayer that he wouldn't come in. Right now she didn't have the strength to face anyone. To her relief, he didn't. Janice must have been waiting on the porch, because it was only a couple of minutes before Callie heard the car leaving.

She and Morgan were alone in the house. Closing her eyes, she remembered the first night he had been there as John Smith. There had been an electricity in the air, now there was only a heavy stillness. Not exactly a stillness, she corrected as the sound of footsteps coming toward the kitchen reached her. Bracing herself, she turned to see Morgan enter.

"I'm leaving," he announced brusquely, coming to a halt in the doorway. "I told Janice to fly directly back to California when she finished visiting her son. Tomorrow I'll pack up our things. I've arranged to stay at Doc's place tonight. I'm sure you'll be happier here alone with your phantoms."

Alone. She suddenly saw herself living out her life in a cold, solitary existence. A chill shook her. Then it happened...the tears began to flow. They ran in rivers down her cheeks.

Morgan stared at her in shock.

Humiliation swept through her. She was crying in front of him. She had taught herself from childhood to keep her emotions to herself and never let anyone know when they were hurting her. Yet, here she was, sobbing openly. "I don't prefer my phantoms," she rasped between clenched teeth. "I did it for you. You should be grateful." She blinked her eyes frantically and brushed at the tears in an effort to stop them.

Anger replaced his shock. "Grateful? You walked out on me and I should be grateful?"

The memory of their parting ran through her mind with sharp clarity. "I don't recall you putting up any argument or raising any objections," she reminded him cuttingly.

"I have my pride," he growled. The contempt returned. "I thought you cared for me. But people who care about someone don't suddenly desert them."

He hated her. She couldn't blame him. Her actions had looked callous. But she'd had good reasons for them. "I did care," she choked out in her defense. A hopelessness washed over her. Talking about it wouldn't change things. Her past was her past. It couldn't be changed. Besides, whatever tender feelings he'd had for her were dead now. A tear dripped from her jaw. She was making a fool of herself! She had to get away. She started toward the back door.

"No, you don't. Not this time," Morgan growled. Reaching her in four long strides, he closed his hand around her upper arm and jerked her to a halt. "This time you're going to answer a few questions."

The anger in his eyes multiplied her feeling of hopelessness. "It can't change anything."

"Oh, yes it can," he assured her grimly. "It can help me get rid of *my* phantoms." His gaze burned into her as self-directed anger spread across his face. "The truth is that's the real reason I'm here, Callie. I've pushed you out of my mind a thousand times and you keep coming back. I'm here to vanquish you once and for all." His fingers tightened on her arm. "Now, I want to know why I should be so grateful."

The tears had finally stopped. She straightened her shoulders and faced him with as much dignity as she could muster. "Because I would have been an embarrassment to you."

He shook his head as if what she was saying didn't make any sense. "An embarrassment?"

She glared at him in exasperation. Abruptly it occurred to her that maybe he didn't remember. Doc had said he might have lost bits and pieces of his memory. Humiliation swept through her. It had been difficult enough telling him the first time. But it had to be done. "Obviously you don't remember, I'm illegitimate."

He continued to regard her grimly. "I do remember. I also recall that I told you that didn't matter."

How could he be so thickheaded! "Of course it wouldn't matter to John Smith," she pointed out curtly. "He had no past to take me back and introduce me to. We would have started off fresh. But Morgan Evans... that's a whole different story." Her chin threatened to tremble, but she held it firm. "You not only have a family but you're an important, influential man with important, influential friends."

The confusion was gone from his eyes, but the anger was still there. "Your past would not have been an embarrassment to me."

That was easy for him to say now, although reality would have changed his tune quickly enough, she thought bitterly. Jerking free from his hold, she took a step back and faced him. "You have no idea of what it would have been like once people learned the truth about me," she snarled as memories of her childhood flooded into her mind. "There would have been whispers and nudges and giggles behind our backs. I know. I lived through the taunts..." Her voice died away. She'd thought she had put those days of humiliation behind her. But they were still surprisingly near the surface.

"I know that children can be cruel to one another," Morgan conceded. "But you're an adult now."

She glared at him. "Adults can be as cruel as children."

"Some can," he admitted. "But they are small-minded people, trying to make themselves feel better by pointing out what they consider defects in others. Those kinds of people hold no interest for me."

She would like to believe him but she couldn't. "What about your mother?" she questioned cynically.

He scowled. "What has my mother got to do with this?"

"You didn't tell her about my past," Callie elaborated in a voice that called him a hypocrite.

"I didn't tell her because I knew it wouldn't matter to her," he replied.

Again Callie wanted to believe him, but he'd never been the object of ridicule. "You would not be so cavalier once the whispering started," she accused.

Morgan stared at her in angry frustration. "Let's be honest. I'm not the sort of man who would let whispers disturb me, but it's clear that they would disturb you. Obviously your feelings toward me are not strong enough. You'd rather stay here, hiding out with your phantoms, than join me in the real world." As if disgusted with the futility of the situation, he turned and stalked out of the room.

Callie's hands balled into fists as the door swung closed behind him. She'd never considered herself a coward, but maybe that was exactly what she was. She thought of her grandfather's robe. Did she want to spend the rest of her life wrapped in a piece of cloth when she was feeling lonely, or did she want a pair of real arms around her? "Only an idiot would settle for an illusion," she told herself. But was it too late? She ran toward the hall. But as she reached it, she came to an abrupt stop.

Morgan was standing about six feet from the front door. In front of him stood Chester blocking Morgan's exit.

"It's about time you showed yourself," Morgan was saying in an impatient growl.

Chester merely smiled. Seeing Callie, he gave her a wink as if to say, *I stopped him for you.* Then he faded and was gone.

"Guess that clears up the last of the loose ends around here," Morgan muttered to himself.

"I was wondering if this loose end might still have a chance to be a part of your life," Callie spoke up shakily.

Morgan jerked around. He had been so intent on Chester, he hadn't noticed her arrival.

"I don't want to spend my life alone with only memories and ghosts to keep me company," she continued nervously. "I thought I was doing what was right for you. But if you won't mind a few whispers, I can face anything with you beside me."

A slow smile spread across his face. "Is that a proposal, Callie Benson?"

She saw the mischievous glimmer in his eyes, and a warmth spread through her. "Yes."

"Then I accept." Reaching her in two long strides, he drew her into his embrace.

"This is much better than living with a phantom," she murmured against his lips as his body pressed against hers and every inch of the contact sparked currents of excitement.

His hold on her tightened possessively. Lifting his head so that his face was about six inches from hers, he looked down at her grimly. "I want your promise that the next time you decide to do something for which I'm supposed to be grateful, you'll talk to me about it first."

"I promise." Reaching up, she gently traced the taut line of his jaw. "I've been so lonely without you." The thought that she had come very close to never having him hold her again shook her. Winding her arms around his neck, she drew herself up closer to him. "I love you, Morgan Evans."

"And I love you, Callie Benson," he returned with a sincerity that caused her toes to curl with delight.

Smiling softly, she added playfully, "And I do like being in the arms of a flesh-and-blood man."

Laughing gently, he claimed her mouth fully.

*   *   *   *   *

WRITTEN IN THE STARS

Love's in Sight!
THROUGH MY EYES
by Helen R. Myers

Dr. Benedict Collier was the perfect
Virgo—poised, confident, always in
control . . . until an accident left him
temporarily blinded. But nurse Jessica
Holden wasn't about to let Ben languish in
his hospital bed. This was her chance to
make Ben open his eyes to the *love* he'd
resisted for years!

THROUGH MY EYES
by Helen R. Myers . . . coming from
Silhouette Romance this September.
It's WRITTEN IN THE STARS!

Silhouette Romance®

Coming Soon

Fashion A Whole New You.
Win a sensual adventurous
trip for two to Hawaii via
American Airlines®, a
brand-new Ford Explorer
4 × 4 and a $2,000
Fashion Allowance.

Plus, special free gifts* are yours to
Fashion A Whole New You.

From September through November, you can take part in
this exciting opportunity from Silhouette.

Watch for details in September.

* with proofs-of-purchase, plus postage and handling

SLFW-TS